Eliza covered the hand that was holding Bonnie's pink ribbon and gave it a gentle squeeze.

Struggling with his thoughts, Walker raised his eyes to hers again. He could feel her empathy, feel her excitement. It was as if she were telegraphing it to him somehow.

His breath caught in his throat.

Was it the emotion-packed moment that had him hallucinating this way, or was there something about this woman that spoke to him? Something that delved into his innermost being and somehow connected with what he kept hidden there?

He made no movement _____ nd, enjoying, instead _____ ou."

His thanks _____ n't accomplish _____ t to do yet. "Save that for _____ er."

Dear Reader,

Valentine's Day is here this month, and what better way to celebrate the spirit of romance than with six fabulous novels from Silhouette Intimate Moments? Kathleen Creighton's *The Awakening of Dr. Brown* is one of those emotional tours de force that will stay in your mind and your heart long after you've turned the last page. With talent like this, it's no wonder Kathleen has won so many awards for her writing. Join Ethan Brown and Joanna Dunn on their journey into the heart. You'll be glad you did.

A YEAR OF LOVING DANGEROUSLY continues with *Someone To Watch Over Her,* a suspenseful and sensuous Caribbean adventure by Margaret Watson. Award winner Marie Ferrarella adds another installment to her CHILDFINDERS, INC. miniseries with *A Hero in Her Eyes,* a real page-turner of a romance. Meet the second of bestselling author Ruth Langan's THE SULLIVAN SISTERS in *Loving Lizbeth*—and look forward to third sister Celeste's appearance next month. Reader favorite Rebecca Daniels is finally back with *Rain Dance,* a gripping amnesia story. And finally, check out *Renegade Father* by RaeAnne Thayne, the stirring tale of an irresistible Native American hero and a lady rancher.

All six of this month's books are guaranteed to keep you turning pages long into the night, so don't miss a single one. And be sure to come back next month for more of the best and most exciting romantic reading around—right here in Silhouette Intimate Moments.

Enjoy!

Leslie J. Wainger
Executive Senior Editor

Please address questions and book requests to:
Silhouette Reader Service
U.S.: 3010 Walden Ave., P.O. Box 1325, Buffalo, NY 14269
Canadian: P.O. Box 609, Fort Erie, Ont. L2A 5X3

MARIE
FERRARELLA

A Hero in
Her Eyes

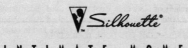

Silhouette®

INTIMATE MOMENTS™

Published by Silhouette Books

America's Publisher of Contemporary Romance

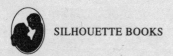

SILHOUETTE BOOKS

ISBN 0-373-27129-8

A HERO IN HER EYES

Copyright © 2001 by Marie Rydzynski-Ferrarella

This edition published by arrangement with Harlequin Books S.A.

® and TM are trademarks of Harlequin Books S.A., used under license.
Trademarks indicated with ® are registered in the United States Patent
and Trademark Office, the Canadian Trade Marks Office and in other
countries.

Visit Silhouette at www.eHarlequin.com

Printed in U.S.A.

To Jessi,
The heart is an incredible muscle. It bounces back,
and to remain healthy it needs to be exercised.
If at first...
Love,
Mom

Prologue

She was running, running because someone was after her.

She ran blindly through grass that came up to her hips, threatening to trip her as she made her way to where the oak tree stood. Her heart was pounding so hard, it blotted out the sounds of the meadow.

Reaching the oak, she stopped, panting and pressing her cheek against the coarse bark as if it were an old friend. Her only friend.

She had no friends.

She wasn't allowed to have any. He wouldn't let her. She wasn't allowed to talk with anyone, couldn't play with anyone.

She was afraid of him.

The lady tried to be nice, but she was afraid of her,

too. Afraid of the wild look in the lady's eyes. Afraid of those big hands that stroked her too hard, hugged her too close. Afraid of the lady who called her a name that wasn't hers.

He was coming. She could feel it. Deep down in her chest, she could feel it.

Daddy, where are you? Come find me. Please!

And then she heard him.

Heard him calling her. Calling that name he told her to answer to.

"Miranda, where the hell are you?"

Hiding by the tree, she squeezed her eyes tightly shut and wished she could disappear.

But she didn't disappear.

And he found her.

She whimpered as hands reached out and roughly snatched her from the ground.

Dragging her away.

Back to the ugly house.

Eliza bolted upright, drenched in perspiration despite the chill in the air.

Slowly, the things around her came into focus. She was in bed, in her own room.

Safe.

Gasping for air to steady her erratic pulse, she leaned forward and dragged her hand through her hair. That was the fifth time she'd had that dream in as many nights. Wasn't it ever going to stop?

She sighed and leaned her forehead against her knees, hugging her legs to her. She knew the answer to that question. It wasn't going to stop.

Not until she figured out who the little girl was.

Chapter 1

"No offense, Eliza, but you look like hell."

As the words penetrated her brain, Eliza glanced up from the computer screen. Her eyes felt dry from staring at Internet photographs for the last two-and-a-half hours. Ever since six this morning.

Unable to sleep, she'd come in early and planted herself in front of her computer, determined to put a name to the face in her dreams. She'd looked up the National Center for Missing and Exploited Children Web site, the first resource everyone at the agency turned to.

Right now, the faces she was looking at were all beginning to run together in her mind.

Holding back the sigh that had taken possession of her, Eliza massaged her temples where a serious headache was starting to take hold.

Nevertheless, the smile she offered Cade Townsend, the founder of ChildFinders, Inc., was genuine. "No offense taken."

"When did you last get a good night's sleep?" Cade crossed his arms before him as he regarded her face more closely. "And if you don't mind my asking, just what are you doing here so early? Don't clairvoyants sleep?"

"On occasion." Eliza deflected his question neatly. "And I could ask the same of you," she added, flipping to the next file.

"You could," he allowed affably. "And my answer would be that sometimes I like coming in while the office is still quiet, before the day and chaos catch up to it. It gives me the illusion that I'm actually on top of things." And then he smiled. "And I'm here because my wife said I was driving her crazy."

Amusement highlighted Eliza's fine-boned face as she welcomed a respite from the darker things that occupied her thoughts. "Oh?"

"McKayla says I was hovering around her and her swollen belly like a starving man watching the timer on a stove, waiting for the roast to be ready." Cade paused, then asked, "You don't, by any chance, have any clue as to when Mike might give—"

She'd wondered what had taken Cade so long to ask. There were those who regarded her and her gift to be in the same realm as carnival performers, as turbaned pretenders who could tell a fortune or suddenly "see" the future at the turn of a coin. She'd grown up with people like that coming in and out of her life.

But Cade Townsend, as well as the others here at ChildFinders, had given her nothing but the utmost respect, treating her not like an oddity, an anomaly of nature, but a woman with something very real, very tangible to offer the organization. Cade was the first to cite her hard work and dedicated professionalism. That she was one of the few true clairvoyants, he'd once said, was only a plus, but not her greatest asset.

She liked Cade. He made her feel as if she actually belonged.

Eliza laughed. "I'm not sure that McKayla would welcome my touching her belly, trying to divine an answer for you."

She knew he'd seen her do it before, touch things that belonged to a kidnapped victim, trying to commune with an essence the rest of them could not fathom. Though McKayla liked Eliza, Eliza could just hear his wife's very vocal reaction to that.

Cade waved away his unfinished request. "You're absolutely right. I've never seen a woman get so testy before. Not that she was the most easygoing woman to begin with, but she was at least reasonable," he confided in an uncustomary moment of intimacy.

She understood exactly what he was saying. Eliza stretched, leaning back in the chair. Her back ached. "They're called hormones, Cade. We're all blessed— or cursed—with them to some extent. Hers are just a little out of sync right now."

He seemed to appreciate the charitable explanation, and laughed softly. "Now there's an understatement."

About to leave, Cade paused, curious. He looked over Eliza's shoulder at the monitor. They were all acutely familiar at the agency with the Web site she was looking at. Ever changing, ever growing, the Web site was filled with a preponderance of photographs of smiling children of all ages. Children who had vanished out of lives that had been carefully or carelessly laid out, breaking the hearts of those who cared about them.

From the looks of it, Eliza had gone through at least two-thirds of the listings. He vaguely recognized the face she was looking at. The girl had been on the site ever since he'd founded ChildFinders, when his own son had been kidnapped. Darin had eventually been found. This girl had not.

He rested his hand on the monitor. "You didn't tell me you're working on a new case." His only rules were that he be kept apprised of every new case that came in and that the first client interview be taped to prevent any misunderstandings down the line.

Eliza half turned in her chair to look at him. "That's because I'm not. At least, not exactly."

"Can you get a little more specific than that?"

Though Cade was an incredibly understanding man Eliza had a great deal of respect for, a lifetime of having to defend herself, of being thought of as "the different one'' had her unconsciously bracing herself for unpleasantness.

''There's this child in my dreams—'' She stopped, wondering how to phrase what she needed to say.

Cade's eyes were nothing if not kind. ''Go on,'' he coaxed quietly, interested.

Feeling suddenly self-conscious, she gave a seemingly careless shrug. ''You don't have time to listen.''

''Sure I do. It's early, remember?'' Cade leaned a hip against the side of her desk. ''And my last case wrapped up five days ago.''

Okay, he asked for it, Eliza thought, taking a breath. ''There's this child. She's running through a field. There's tall, tall grass that makes it hard for her to run, but she pushes on anyway. She's about four, maybe five, blond, green-eyed and very frightened. She keeps calling out to her father to come find her. Except he doesn't.''

Listening intently, Cade nodded. ''Anything else?''

She closed her eyes for a moment to focus. ''I see a farmhouse in the background.'' Eliza opened her eyes again and looked at Cade. ''It has that old, run-down look, like one of those places you see in those old documentaries about the Depression.''

''Abandoned?''

She'd gotten that feeling, but she couldn't be sure. It was the little girl who had held all of her attention. ''Maybe.''

''What makes you think the little girl is real?'' Cade asked. His tone was tactful, kind. ''I mean, she might be a fabrication of your mind, a holdover from a movie you saw or television program you caught, or even a composite from your past cases.''

It was a question she'd already asked herself. ''No, she's real. I know it.'' Eliza was as certain of that as she was of who and what she was. ''Someone's taken her, I'm sure of it. I've had this dream over and over again, Cade. In the last week, I've had it for five nights straight.'' She looked back at the monitor. The little girl had to be in there somewhere. ''She's real, Cade, and she's out there. Lost. Looking to come home.''

''Anything I can do?'' Cade asked.

Until she found a match somehow, there was nothing any of them could do. Eliza sighed. ''You can ask Carrie to buy more coffee when she gets a chance. We're almost out.'' She nodded at the mug on her desk. ''I made a double batch this morning.''

Cade moved away from the desk, inadvertently brushing against Eliza's arm. ''Thanks for the heads-up. I'll be sure to steer clear of it.'' And then he grinned. ''Although Megan will probably tell you it's too weak. If you need any help, let me know.''

The slight contact had created a burst of light within her. Eliza looked at Cade confidently. ''Sure thing, but you'll be too busy.''

''No, I—'' The significance of her words hit him. He realized that he'd accidentally brushed against her. From what she'd told him, he knew that Eliza's insights came at will. Cade looked at her now, his eyes widening. "Really?"

She smiled broadly at him. You'd think this was his first time expecting, instead of a second go-round. "Really."

He crossed back to her, more eager than she'd ever seen him. "When?"

"This afternoon," she answered with no hesitation. In her mind, she'd seen the baby, seen one of the assisting nurses recording the time. "3:32."

"3:32," he echoed like a man in a trance. He wasn't skeptical, he really wasn't, but he would have been less than human if he didn't ask, "But two minutes ago, you said you didn't know."

She knew he wasn't challenging her. At times, this whole thing left her in awe herself.

"Two minutes ago, I didn't. Like I've told you, I have no control over this. Things come to me. Or they don't. All I can do is pass on the information when I get it." Eliza had made her peace with this, though there were times when it still proved frustrating to her. "I'm not much more than a conduit."

"You're a lot more than that." Cade squeezed her hand, grateful for her information and for the fact that worrying about McKayla would be behind him soon. As of yesterday, his wife was officially three weeks overdue. "Thanks. And if you need any help with that—" he nodded at the computer monitor "—I can ask Chad if he has any extra—"

"Thanks, but I don't think anyone else is going to

be able to help, Cade—not yet, at any rate. I've only got a vague picture of the little girl in my mind, and right now, I'm the only one who would even recognize her.''

"What we need is a good sketch artist as part of the firm,'' Cade commented, leaving. "Well, don't tire yourself out,'' he warned. "I don't like my operatives dead on their feet, and you're not going to help that little girl's case any by turning into a zombie.''

"Zombie, freak. You're a freak, that's what you are. Why the hell can't you be normal, like other little girls?''

The voice echoed in her brain as loudly now as it had any one of the number of times her father had shouted those words at her. They'd come from his own frustration over not being able to understand what was going on with his only child.

He'd been a simple man who understood simple things. His own daughter had seemed like something out of a science-fiction movie to him. He was incapable of bridging the gap that existed between them. After her mother died, that gap had only grown wider.

It had been hard on her father, she told herself now—as she had countless times before in an attempt to smother the hurt his words generated—having a daughter who was different, a daughter with "the gift'' as her great-aunt called it.

She'd spent a good portion of her early years wishing the "gift'' had been returnable. At the time, she would have given anything to be just like everyone else, just like the "normal" girls her father was forever pointing out to her as a goal to strive for. Being a seer, someone in touch with other people's pasts and futures, and having those timelines indiscriminately mix with her own present without warning, was more of a curse to her than a gift.

It had certainly been a cross to bear that had made her fearful—until her mother's aunt, who had endured the same fears, the same trials, had taken her aside to explain the good that could be done with the power she had.

"To ignore it is a sin, Eliza. You have to find a way to use it, to help people. That's why the good Lord picked you. He knew you could do good with it. Don't disappoint Him, Eliza. And most of all, don't disappoint yourself."

So here she was, with little to no sleep, staring bleary-eyed at an endless series of photographs of children's faces. Looking for one in particular. Trying to make sense out of her gift and find a reason why she was dreaming of a child she did not know.

It wasn't the first time, but that didn't make it any less frustrating, any less challenging.

Behind her, the door to her office closed softly. Eliza blinked, trying to refocus her eyes. Trying to see the girl she'd been missing. The one she was certain was in the computer database somewhere. With a sigh, she reached for the coffee that had grown cold.

About to push away from the computer to take a

breather, thinking she might need some distance before she continued the search, something compelled her to look at the next photograph on file.

Eliza's mouth fell open.

Afraid to blink, to look away, she pressed a key to zoom in. "There you are."

She had no idea why she was surprised—not when the feeling came, the one that led her to places she would never have thought of going. The feeling that went hand in hand with being clairvoyant. That forced her into people's faces with bravado when she would much rather have retreated.

Her body at attention, Eliza moved her chair closer to the monitor. "So, hello," she whispered to the little girl in the photograph. The little girl in her dream. "I've been looking for you."

The moment she'd clicked on the file, seen the small, animated face, a sliver of the dream flashed through her mind's eye, confirming the identification.

If she concentrated very intently, Eliza could almost swear she heard someone calling for the child. *Bonnie.*

An eagerness swept over Eliza, erasing her tiredness, erasing everything but the desire to find this child in real life, just the way she had on the Web site.

Quickly she printed out the page with the information. She needed to contact the family.

"Hang on, Bonnie," she murmured. "We'll find you."

* * *

He'd discovered that grief, like the possessions scattered within a child's room, could be boxed up and put out of sight. But unlike the boxes that held his daughter's clothes and toys, the box that his grief was stored in would periodically appear right before him, without warning, tripping him. Bringing a pain with it that was almost insurmountable.

But he dealt with it.

He had no choice.

He'd made his peace and moved on, not once but twice. Moved on and kept moving. Moving so the box wouldn't trip him. Moving so that he could pretend he was among the living instead of the walking wounded. Or worse, the walking dead.

And in moving, he went through the motions of living. Those who knew him were taken in by the facade, the performance, and believed Walker Banacek to be a man who had healed from profound wounds that would have felled a lesser person. He had survived his tragedies and found the strength to continue. There was nothing more admirable than that.

It wasn't even remotely true, but he pretended, for his own sanity, that it was. It was how he got through each day and forced himself to get up each morning. All pretense.

In place of a family life, he dedicated himself to his work. The irony of it never failed to strike him. He dealt with security. Computer security. He'd developed software that kept computers and sensitive information safe—while the security of his family had been breached.

He was the first one in the corporate offices in the morning, the last one to leave at night. Weekends would find him there, as well, working so he wouldn't have to think, wouldn't have to feel. He anesthetized himself, and for the most part it worked.

Until he tripped over the box again. Always without warning.

Today had been just that kind of day. He'd tripped over the box, releasing a plethora of memories, of emotions, none of which he was capable of dealing with. Tripped, because today his daughter would have been six years old.

Someone in the office down the hall had been celebrating a birthday. An off-key rendition of "Happy Birthday" was all that was necessary; the thoughts had hooked up to one another instantly, bringing him back to the emotional abyss he'd struggled, time and again, to flee.

Worn from the inside out, Walker made it home, entering the house where lights went on automatically at sundown so that he didn't have to contend with shadows. So that his mind wouldn't play tricks on him and make him believe he was seeing an elfin, dancing figure out of the corner of his eye.

Bonnie used to love to dance around the room, pretending to be a ballerina. He'd bought her toe shoes for her fourth birthday, over his wife's protests. Bonnie had worn them everywhere in place of her shoes. She'd had them on the day she disappeared.

The thought of dinner came and went in a single heartbeat. He wasn't hungry. He never was anymore. Eating was just something he did to keep going. He vaguely remembered having lunch, and decided that would be sufficient to sustain him until breakfast tomorrow. If he remembered to eat then. A housekeeper came daily, to wipe away the cobwebs and prepare simple meals that were hardly touched. Life went on, in a way.

Walker debated turning on the television set, not because there was anything he wanted to watch, but because the sound of it might interfere with this overwhelming loneliness tripping over the box had triggered.

He didn't like being alone, but in all this time, he couldn't make himself allow anyone in to witness the pain he was grappling with.

Riffling through the mail on the counter that the housekeeper had brought in earlier in the day, he heard the doorbell. Ignoring it, he sorted the mail into two piles. Everything that wasn't a bill went into the pile to be thrown away.

The doorbell rang again. And then again, defying his determination to ignore it. He stopped sorting. Whoever was on the other side of his door obviously refused to accept the obvious—that he wasn't about to answer.

The ringing continued at one-minute intervals.

They weren't going to go away. There was a time when he would have flown to the door at the first indication of a knock, picked up the phone before the first ring was completed, praying each time that it was someone with news that Bonnie had been found.

But each time, it wasn't.

Instead, there'd been a bevy of reporters, a squadron of ghouls calling with "sightings" of his daughter, all feeding off the situation. He'd gone on countless emotional roller-coaster rides, only to be disappointed over and over again. Until he'd shut himself off completely, knowing that the call, the knock he was waiting for, would never come.

Expecting no one, angry at being invaded, Walker crossed to the front door. He yanked it open and fairly growled out the single word.

"Yes?"

Startled, Eliza almost took a step back from the man in the doorway. It wasn't his expression that had her temporarily thinking of retreat, or even the way he'd snapped out the word in something far less than an actual greeting. Rather, it was the aura of pain she felt hovering around him that had unsettled her. Pain so vividly present, she felt she could literally reach out and touch it with her hand.

He was a man who had suffered a great deal, and her heart went out to him. He had Bonnie's eyes, she thought, looking at him.

"Mr. Banacek?"

"Yes?" This time, the word came out a little more

civilized sounding, though it was by no means intended to be friendly.

He wanted to be left alone. Alone to repackage the box and find some way to store it away again. It was hard enough to find a place for himself tonight without having to deal with some wispy dark-blond stranger who looked as if the wind had literally blown her to his doorstep.

"My name is Eliza Eldridge. I'd like to speak to you about Bonnie."

His jaw tightened so rigidly, had it been made out of glass, Eliza was certain it would have shattered.

"What about her?"

"I believe she's still alive." In her entire experience, she'd never found an easy way to say this. "I've had this dream about her—"

His eyes darkened to the color of a storm. The next moment, he'd slammed the door shut in her face.

Chapter 2

The ringing began again, more insistent than the last time.

Walker felt himself beginning a not-so-slow burn. Didn't these people have lives? Didn't they have anything better to do than torment people touched by tragedy?

He strode back to the door, growing angrier with the woman leaning on his bell with every step he took.

"Go away, Ms. Eldridge," he shouted through the door. He made no attempt to sound civil. At this point, he just wanted her to get out of his life. "I'm not about to talk to you."

Eliza placed her outstretched hand on the door, wishing there was some way to touch the man behind it. Wishing she could make Walker Banacek understand and accept what it was that she wanted to do for him. But this part had never come about easily. It wasn't quite like tilting at windmills, but it came close. People regarded clairvoyants as something between certified lunatics and fairy folk.

"Just give me a few minutes of your time to explain, please."

The door didn't open.

"If you don't leave now," he called to her, "I'll call the police."

If he thought that was a threat, he was going to be disappointed, she thought. She'd been subjected to far worse. "Ask for Lieutenant Trent Lanihan. He'll vouch for me."

For a moment there was nothing but silence, and she thought that perhaps he had walked away, after all. And then, to her surprise, the door opened, but not enough to allow her to come in.

"Look, trust me, I've heard it all," Walker snapped coldly as he stood in the doorway. "So you can take your crystal ball, your tarot cards, your channeling persona, or whatever the hell you claim to use to bilk people out of their money and prey on their paltry hopes, and get the hell off my doorstep because I promise you, I am not in the mood for whatever bill of goods it is you're trying to sell me."

But before Walker could close the door on her again, Eliza wedged her body into the doorway, deterring his attempts to throw her out. He would have to do it bodily, or be forced to listen to her.

When he glared at her incredulously, she met his gaze not defiantly, but with such understanding that it took his breath away. Stunned, he stopped holding the door firmly in place and listened.

"I don't use a crystal ball, tarot cards or a channeling persona," she told him in a soft voice meant to inspire confidence and soothe an impassioned beast. Her mouth curved slightly; she knew exactly what he was thinking. "I'm not a quack, Mr. Banacek. I have no explanation for my abilities, I only know that there are times when I'm made aware of things that other people aren't, and at times I can see things that other people don't."

He sincerely doubted that. She didn't "see" things; what she accomplished she did with hypnosis. In his opinion, there was no other explanation for why he'd momentarily ceased pushing her out. No other explanation why he wasn't pushing her out this second. It had to be hypnosis. One look into her eyes would convince anyone of that. They were a light shade of blue, so light that it made him think of the nylon used in making translucent nightgowns. Even now they seemed to be invading his very mind.

He blinked, rousing himself. Whatever tricks she was attempting to pull, they weren't going to work on him. He'd been through too much already. "Go away," he ordered sternly.

Eliza hated being put in the position of forcing herself on someone, but this was too important for her to turn away. A child's life could be hanging in the balance.

"Not yet, Mr. Banacek, not until you hear me out. When I'm finished, if you still want me to leave, I will. No calls to the police will be necessary."

Walker was torn. He didn't like being played for a fool, but he had to admit that no matter how hard he tried to smother it, to bury it, there was still a small part of him that clung to irrational hope, hope that flew in the face of all the statistics to the contrary. Hope of finding Bonnie.

His eyes held hers. Then, after a beat, he opened the door a little wider. But his body remained in the way, blocking access to his house. He wasn't about to let her mistake this for an invitation.

"What is this to you?"

He had a right to question. "A lost child, Mr. Banacek," she replied softly. "What is it to you?"

How *dare* she? His eyes dissolved into angry slits as he glared at her. "A trick, a ploy. I don't know whether you're a reporter, a tragedy groupie or just a crackpot—"

And he had been besieged by all of them, Eliza thought. In large numbers. There was nothing she could do about that. But to have his help, she needed to change his mind. "There is a fourth choice."

"Which is?" His tone was guarded. Hypnotically beautiful eyes not withstanding, he wasn't about to be suckered into anything. Those days were gone.

Her eyes looked straight into him. "That I'm on the level."

Looking away, Walker laughed shortly. Even if he might once have been inclined to believe the kind of nonsense she was spouting, he'd learned his lesson the hard way. His wife had paid clairvoyants to help. All they had done was help separate Rachel from her money. Bonnie was dead and he had to accept that. *Had* accepted it. He wasn't about to retrace his steps or retract his decision, the decision it had taken him months of soul-wrenching searching to reach.

He placed his hand on the door, ready to push it closed again. "Sorry, I don't believe in things that go bump in the night."

Her hand touched his as she moved to stop him. A volley of lights blazed before her eyes. House lights. Bedroom lights. "Is that why you keep the lights on at night?"

Because he couldn't summon a single word to answer her with, Walker stared at her in stunned silence.

"When you go to sleep at night," she continued in a gentle voice, knowing that he desperately needed comfort, needed hope, not someone who raised her voice to match his in a dual of words, "is that why you don't turn off the lights?"

"How did you know...?" For the briefest of moments, Walker actually entertained the thought that she was on the level. And then he came to his senses. There was a logical explanation, there always was.

He just had to look for it. "You read that somewhere, didn't you?"

Although, in all honesty, he didn't remember ever telling anyone that, not even his sister. It was just something between him and the memory of the child he still carried in his heart. The child who was no more.

"No." The single word was devoid of guile. "Until this morning, I didn't even know who you were." She'd missed the news media's coverage of the tragedy, missed the stories on page one and then page three until they had worked their way to the back of the newspaper. "I wasn't in the city the month your daughter was kidnapped. I was in Georgia." Holding the hand of a man who had never accepted her. Holding his hand as he lay dying.

Eliza pushed the memory away. She was here to offer her help because Bonnie Banacek was missing, not to remember things that caused her pain. Pain only interfered with her ability to see things clearly.

Walker crossed his arms before his chest, a physically and emotionally immovable force. "Uh-huh. And just what is it that brings you to my door now?"

He didn't believe her, she thought. She'd caught him off guard with her question about the lights, shaken him up, but he still clung to his disbelief. In his place, maybe she'd do the same.

All she could so was tell him the truth. "I've been having dreams about Bonnie. I think she's using me to get a message to you."

A sneer crept into his eyes, over his lips. He'd caught her in a lie. "I thought you said you didn't 'channel.'"

"It's not channeling," she corrected gently. As far as she knew, that had never happened to her. "Channeling a spirit supposedly involves someone who's passed on. Your daughter is very much alive, Mr. Banacek."

Walker wanted to shout at her, to shake her until she recanted. He didn't know how, but he managed to hold on to his temper. "Oh, and I have your guarantee on this, Miss—" He broke off in frustration.

"Eldridge," she repeated quietly. "Eliza Eldridge." Opening her purse, she took out a business card and handed it to him.

Now they were getting to it, he thought cynically. The pitch. He glanced down at the card.

"ChildFinders, Inc.?" Angry, he shoved the card back into her hand. "What is this, some alternative form of ambulance chasing?"

She had no choice but to take the card back. "No, that's just a number where you can reach me during the day." And she hoped he would. "This has nothing to do with the agency."

He was going to close the door, she saw it in his eyes. Eliza placed her hand on his arm in a silent entreaty. "The dream keeps recurring," she told him. "I went to the National Center for Missing and Exploited Children Web site and looked for someone who resembled the girl in my dream."

A very convincing cover story, but that was all it was: a story. A one-story-fits-all with no truth to it. He made no effort to hide his contempt. "Is that how you drum up business?"

She could almost feel the wall of hostility he'd erected around himself. "No, we have no need to drum up business. Sadly, there's more than enough to go around. We get calls to search for missing children from all over the country."

"Then why are you bothering me?" he demanded, suddenly drained. Too drained to even pretend to be polite. "Go answer them and leave me alone."

She tried to stop him, but even as she did, she felt it was futile. He'd already made up his mind. "Please, Mr. Banacek, I know I can help. I just need you to let me see her room, touch some of her things."

He wasn't about to parade Bonnie's things in front of a stranger, no matter how altruistic she pretended to be. "No. Now go back and pull your innocent act on someone else. I've been through it all and I'm not buying."

One swift movement was all it took. The door was closed.

Eliza looked down at the card still in her hand. She knew that even if she rang the bell again, Walker Banacek wouldn't answer. Wouldn't listen to what she had to tell him. Wouldn't be swayed. He'd isolated himself so far away from hope that right now, there was no way to reach him. She needed something tangible to show him, to make him change his mind.

After debating for a moment, she took her business card and inserted it between the double doors just above the doorknob. Walking away, she glanced back at the card. She had no way of knowing whether he'd take it when he opened the door tomorrow morning.

Not for the first time, she wished her insight would allow her some way to access it at will.

But she was as much in the dark about what caused the visions, the sudden rifts in her own present, as most people. All she knew was that it worked when it worked.

Glancing again over her shoulder as she walked back to her car, she thought of the man holed up inside the big house.

Despite his pain, Walker Banacek wasn't the important one here, she reminded herself. It was his daughter. Eliza couldn't lose sight of that.

Things would probably be a great deal easier for her if the girl's father gave her his help, but one way or another, she intended to try to find the lost girl. She knew she wouldn't get any sleep unless she did at least that much.

He hardly slept.

As he got out of bed the next day, Walker blamed his endless night on the woman who had come to his door, offering to do magic for him. Offering to find a child whom he had forced himself to accept was forever out of his life. Several times in the wee hours of his night, he damned the petite woman for disrupting the life he struggled to keep orderly.

If he were honest with himself, he thought as he got dressed, his life was in a continuous state of disruption and had been for the past two years.

Nothing was ever going to be the same again. The ache that had suddenly surged through him threatened to undo him completely. He banked it down.

She had brought it to a head, he thought angrily, this Eliza Eldridge and her claims of clairvoyance. It didn't take a clairvoyant to see that she was just out to make some money for herself and this so-called organization she belonged to.

Well, she wouldn't be making it off him, or his grief. He wouldn't allow it.

Too agitated to eat, Walker deliberately walked past his refrigerator without stopping. Crossing to the front door, he decided to pick up a coffee on the way to the office.

Maybe coffee would wake him up.

A small, pearl-colored rectangle floated to the step by his foot as he opened the door. He stooped to pick it up, then cursed softly.

She'd left her card.

What part of ''no'' didn't she understand?

About to throw the card away, Walker stopped and looked again. Changing his mind, he pocketed it. He'd call his lawyer this morning when he got a chance and tell Jason to look into getting a restraining order against this Eliza Eldridge and ChildFinders, Inc. Undoubtedly, she didn't give up easily.

There was something in her eyes...

He didn't have time to think about a nicely packaged huckster. Didn't have time to think about anything that had to do with Bonnie and the life he'd had before everything had turned pitch black for him.

Forcing himself to think of nothing but the work piled up on his desk in the office, Walker hurried to his car.

"She's on the level, Walker."

Walker frowned, wondering if the connection had somehow gotten scrambled. Hand on the phone receiver, he sat up in the rigid office chair. "What? Aren't you too old to believe in witches and women who cast spells?"

There was a deep chuckle on the other end of the line. "God, I hope I'm never too old to believe in women who cast spells." Jason's comment was directed at Walker as his lifelong friend rather than as the client who kept him and his law office on year-round retainer. "But I looked into her just as you asked me to yesterday, and Eliza Eldridge isn't any of the things you accused her of being. As far as the police are concerned, she's the real McCoy. She's helped solve several prominent kidnapping cases here, in Texas and in Georgia."

Walker found that impossible to believe. "By doing what, looking into her crystal ball?"

Of the two of them, Walker had been the more practical one, even as far back as grammar school. His only dreams had revolved around the creation of the company he now headed.

"Hey, even Shakespeare said there were more things in heaven and earth than we could ever possibly understand."

"Yeah, like people who prey on other people's grief."

"Hey, you'll get no argument from me, Walker. I've come across plenty of those in my time. All I'm saying is that it looks as if Eliza Eldridge and the agency she works for are one of the good guys. From everything I've read, ChildFinders, Inc. has a one-hundred-percent track record for recovering the children they're hired to find," Jason said.

"And you don't find that somehow suspect?"

"There's a place for everything in this world, Walker. Even miracles. If she came looking for you with some kind of message, I say go for it. What have you got to lose?"

"What have I got to lose? How about the bits and pieces of me that I've managed to pull together over the past two years? Damn it, Jason..."

Jason felt for Walker, he really did. He'd been there for him, as much as Walker would allow anyone to be there for him, and had seen what the kidnapping had done to him. And to Walker's wife, Rachel. One tragedy had begat another. "Yeah, I know."

"No, you don't," Walker said with finality. "You

don't know. You couldn't possibly know until it's happened to you what it feels like to lose your little girl. To finally have to admit to yourself that there's no hope, that she's never going to come back, never going to throw those little arms around you and hug you as if you're the most important person in the world. Never feel those tiny little lips on your cheek when you've won her heart because you bought her a stupid pair of pink toe shoes—''

Abruptly, Walker stopped, knowing he'd said too much, had gotten too angry at a friend whose only sin was in wanting to help.

When he spoke again, his voice quavered. ''I just don't know if I can go through it all again, Jase. I don't know if I could live with myself.''

''Could you live with yourself if you turned your back on this, knowing there might be some chance, however slim, that you could find Bonnie? And that you passed it up?''

Walker made no answer.

He didn't have to.

There were no two ways about it. Savannah Walters was an absolute gem. Eliza wondered what the firm had done without her before Sam had found her daughter, married her and subsequently talked her into leaving her job and coming to work for Child-Finders. The woman was an absolute whiz at the computer. More to the point, she knew her way around what was, to Eliza, the mysterious world of the Internet. Savannah could uncover information in seconds where it would have taken her weeks, Eliza marveled as she went over the stacks of files, clippings and random bits of information Savannah had assembled for her.

Specifically, she'd asked Savannah to see if she could dig up any information regarding the Banacek kidnapping. Savannah had unearthed old news articles dealing with the kidnapping and any bodies that had subsequently turned up fitting Bonnie's general physical description over a nine-state area. She'd also asked for the names and known whereabouts of any registered child molesters.

It was a humbling mound of information, but Eliza intended to do it all justice. Maybe reading the files would trigger something for her, she thought. She felt she owed it to Bonnie, no matter what the girl's father thought of her.

"Hey, there's the brand-new Daddy now." Eliza heard Megan Andreini Wichita crow almost right outside her door. It sounded as if Megan was hugging Cade. "How does it feel?"

Cade had taken the day before off to be with his wife, after having spent the previous evening coaching her through labor and delivery.

"I'll let you know when and if I get some sleep. Right now, I'm so tired I feel like I'm walking around in someone else's dream." He stopped to pop his head into Eliza's office. "You were right. Mike had the baby at 3:32. A beautiful baby girl." Reaching into his jacket pocket, he pulled out the instamatic photo he'd taken and passed it around for the women to see. "Her face's a little flattened right now, but—"

"Her face," Eliza said, taking the photograph from him to get a better look, "is absolutely perfect. And so is she." She handed the photograph over to Savannah. "You must be very, very proud."

Normally a man of few words, he wasn't given to bragging. "Just relieved it's over."

"Hey, it's not over, Papa," Savannah, the mother of two children herself, told him affectionately. "You should know that. It's not over for eighteen years. And even then, I hear it doesn't stop."

Megan handed the photograph back to the man she had originally met when she'd come as an FBI agent to question him about his missing son. "Boy, you people really know how to sell motherhood."

"Nothing better in this world," Savannah swore solemnly.

Megan chewed on her lower lip, seeming uncustomarily uncertain. "That's good." She took a deep breath as the others looked at her questioningly. "Because I think I'm on my way."

"My God, really?" Savannah asked.

Megan had only been back to the office for a couple of days. She and her husband, Garrett, had finally managed to coordinate their schedules to take a long overdue honeymoon.

"Wow, you certainly know how to end off a honeymoon right," Cade commented.

Eliza threw her arms around Megan, then stepped back. Megan looked at her with an unspoken question in her eyes. Eliza nodded with a smile. "Yes, you are."

Megan squealed and hugged her hard.

Chapter 3

The sleek, gray Jaguar slipped into a spot that availed itself of the shade from one of the older benjamina trees that framed the perimeter of the parking lot closest to the office building.

His palm resting on the hand brake, Walker paused to gather his thoughts as he looked out at the building through the tinted window.

He wasn't certain exactly what he'd been expecting. He supposed that in his mind, he'd thought any place that numbered a clairvoyant among its active employees would look like something out of a second-rate, melodramatic movie, maybe even one of those simpleminded screamers that dealt with the supernatural. The entrance to the building would come with a fog machine billowing out dry ice to create the proper surreal atmosphere.

That ChildFinders, Inc. had an address that put it squarely in the heart of one of Bedford's most upscale business plazas was almost as encouraging as the verbal voucher Jason had given him over the phone regarding the agency's sterling reputation.

A place that dedicated itself to finding missing children—and continually succeeding at it, if he was to believe the publicity—couldn't be all bad, he told himself.

Braced for anything, Walker got out of his car and entered the building.

ChildFinders's offices took up the entire top floor of the five-story building. The rent on that had to be a pretty penny, Walker mused, getting into the elevator whose outer wall was made of Plexiglas. It allowed him a view of the parking lot he'd just left as he got in.

If the rent was high, that meant that altruistic publicity notwithstanding, ChildFinders had to charge astronomical rates to stay ahead of the game, he decided, pressing for the fifth floor.

Not that money was a problem for him. It hadn't been for almost ten years now. It was everything else that had become a problem, Walker thought darkly, watching the cars below become progressively smaller as he drew closer to the fifth floor.

When the elevator came to a smooth halt, Walker found himself stepping out into a tastefully decorated reception area. Looking around, he half expected the walls to be decorated with prominent citizens and ce-

lebrities the agency had helped, a visual testimonial
to its incredible success rate.

Again, he was wrong.

Instead of photographs of grateful parents, there
was a gallery of children's photographs. Children, he
assumed, that the different operatives had recovered
and reunited with their families. Beyond that were
several large, colorful pastels scattered about in un-
derstated frames. The two blended in to create an
atmosphere that was at once soothing and brightly
encouraging.

It was a place meant to put a person at their ease,
not impress them.

Good business sense, he noted absently. Whoever
had done this knew what they were doing.

He looked around for someone to talk to.

The young woman behind the reception desk at the
entrance to the offices hardly looked old enough to
be out of high school without a written excuse note
from her mother. He vaguely wondered if she was
one of the agency's success stories.

Approaching the desk, Walker cleared his throat.
He was nervous, he realized. Was he was making
some sort of ridiculous mistake in coming here?

Maybe yes, but Jason was right. If he didn't come
here, if he didn't follow up this absurd—for lack of
a better word—lead, he would always wonder if he'd
turned his back on the only and last chance he would
ever have of finding Bonnie. As far-fetched as this
seemed, he couldn't ignore it.

Walker stopped short of the desk. Somewhere during the ride here from his corporate offices at the other end of Bedford, he realized, he had given himself permission to think of his daughter as being among the living again.

The thought startled him.

He feared that he would live to regret this. But his heart wanted so badly to believe that it was really true—that Bonnie was alive somewhere and that he would find her if only he tried hard enough.

As if he hadn't tried hard before, doing everything in his power, hiring everyone he could...

And it had all come to nothing.

The girl at the reception desk flashed a thousand-watt smile. "May I help you?"

"Is Ms.—" His mind suddenly blank, Walker had to pause and look at the card he'd shoved into his jacket pocket just before he'd gotten out of the Jaguar. Funny, he was usually so good with names. Why did hers keep eluding him? Probably had to do with the fact that he was so skeptical. "Is Ms. Eldridge in?"

She answered his question with a question. "Do you have an appointment?"

"No, I don't. I—"

Fear leaped in from nowhere. Fear of going on the same gut-wrenching roller-coaster ride he'd been on before to the same spirit-destroying destination. Fear of subjecting himself to all the same emotions, to the same heartache.

He just couldn't do it to himself again. Coming here was a mistake.

"Never mind, I'll come back when I have an appointment." Turning abruptly on his heel, Walker started for the elevator.

"You could make one now."

Her words reached him just as he was about to press for the elevator.

It was the same low, melodious voice he'd heard coming from the other side of his front door two days ago. The clairvoyant. He hadn't seen her come out.

Somewhat embarrassed, like a child caught with his hand wedged into the forbidden cookie jar, Walker turned around to discover that Eliza was standing directly behind him.

He hadn't realized she was so delicate looking. She seemed smaller somehow, more petite. Here, on her home territory, she appeared almost elfin. Or maybe it was just his imagination.

Weren't elves the ones who were supposed to grant you wishes when you found them in their own lair? Or was he getting that confused with leprechauns? He wasn't sure. Most of all, he wasn't sure anymore just what he was doing here.

She'd felt his presence. Sitting in her office, poring over information that ultimately might or might not have to do with Bonnie's disappearance, she'd suddenly become aware that something had changed. Walker was entering the building.

It would probably spook him if she told him that,

she thought with a smile. It had taken her a long time to learn exactly what she could share with someone and what she needed to keep to herself, if she didn't want them to think of her in the same belittling way her father had.

She'd ventured out of her office, curious to see if she was right, if she actually had sensed his presence, or if concentrating so hard on recovering Bonnie had made her think Walker had come. She'd certainly been hoping that he would. It would make things a great deal less difficult for her to do her job if she had access to Bonnie's things.

Her job. That was what she'd decided it would be, even as she'd walked away from Walker's closed front door. Her job. Her mission. To find Bonnie, no matter how long it took. She had to.

Eliza took his hand as if she were drawing out a reluctant child, encouraging him to join the others.

It surprised Walker how delicate her fingers felt against his skin.

It was her job to do that, he reminded himself, to distract him so she could take him where she wanted him to go. Because he'd been a hustler in the practical sense of the word all his life, hustling first for supporters, then for clients, for people to recognize his designs, and then finally for financial backing—he'd come to think of the rest of the world in those same terms. People hustling to convince others that they both needed and wanted the goods or services the other had to offer.

In this case, there was no question that he did. *If* the services were really legitimate.

That was the doubting Thomas in him, he thought. The practical side that had come by way of his engineer father. The man who had taught him to test twice before he trusted once.

He had yet to really "test" this Eliza Eldridge and her firm.

"You're in luck—I'm in between cases," Eliza informed him quietly, still holding his hand in hers.

She'd probably say that whether or not it was the truth. "Right, luck."

He was still skeptical. Not that she blamed him. He really hadn't witnessed anything that would make him change his mind. "Don't underestimate luck, Mr. Banacek. It plays a large role in almost everything."

His resistance to the whole ludicrous idea of someone being clairvoyant was beginning to strengthen. It was all he could do to keep the sarcasm bubbling within him to a simmer. He wasn't usually rude, but this had brought out his vulnerability, and he was going to do everything he needed to in order to protect himself.

"So you do what, hand out rabbits' feet to your clients or tell them to gather up a bouquet of four-leaf clovers, just to be on the safe side?"

She'd been subjected to a great deal worse and had long since learned that fear and ignorance colored the way people spoke. And Walker was afraid. Afraid to believe. Afraid to be disappointed. And afraid of finally, unequivocally, giving up.

If he had given up the way he thought he had, he wouldn't have come.

"It's not going to make you feel any better to be antagonistic, Mr. Banacek. I just meant that every decision we make has some effect on the way our individual timelines are formed." She smiled into his eyes, trying to give him some of her faith. "A lot of good things have happened to people because they were in the right place at the right time."

"And a lot of bad things have happened to people because they were in the wrong place at the wrong time," he countered.

There was nothing quite so daunting as when reason joined forces with pessimism, she thought. But she was up to the challenge.

"Still luck," she replied. "Just this time, bad. Would you like to step into my office?"

He glanced toward the elevator. It would still be here later, he reasoned. He could always leave.

"Sure." The shrug was careless. "I'm here, why not?"

Eliza smiled. "Why not, indeed?"

He sounded as if he hadn't made the effort to get behind the wheel of his car and seek out ChildFinders. As if he'd just decided, on a lark, to drop by the offices. But she refrained from pointing that out as she led him down the hall to her office.

The office that she occupied had a view of the

ocean, and in the evening, the sunset. Together, they made for a breathtaking scene—whenever she was in the office to witness it. She was comforted to know that the view was there whenever she was in desperate need of tranquillity.

Eliza paused by her door, waiting for Walker to step through.

"Opened or closed?" She indicated the door.

He was busy looking around. It looked like an ordinary office, much smaller than his. There was no incense; there were no candles, no voodoo masks, not even a cluster of books about out-of-body experiences by ghosts who roam the earth. Instead, the only books she had lined up on the single shelf that ran along the sill of her window concerned investigative techniques. He didn't know whether to be relieved or disappointed.

Maybe he was a little of both. "I'm a private person."

"Closed," she concluded with a nod, shutting the door behind her.

Rounding her desk, she sat down behind it. She would rather have sat beside him, unencumbered by the desk, but she knew that he preferred the traditional. Besides, she knew she still made him uneasy. Gentling techniques took time.

Folding her hands before her, she smiled at him. "I take it I passed muster."

"Excuse me?"

Maybe the term was too old-fashioned for him. It'd

been one her great-aunt liked to use. "You're here. That means you had me and or the agency investigated. I'm just assuming that our passing grade was impressive enough to you to bring you here."

Walker shifted in his chair. More body language for her to read, he upbraided himself. He didn't like being so easy to read. Moving to the edge of his chair, he locked eyes with her. "Do you do that sort of thing all the time?"

"Do what?" she asked.

"Read a person's thoughts?"

Even as he asked the question, Walker didn't know if he actually bought into that on any level. It seemed like a bunch of garbage.

But there was just something about her eyes, about the way she looked at him, *into* him, that made him think Eliza Eldridge could actually see his thoughts if she was so inclined.

Maybe he was losing his mind, he thought. Given the stress he'd been under—and was still under, if he was honest with himself—it was small wonder. Not every man lost his child and then his wife within a few months of each other.

"I can't read a person's thoughts, Mr. Banacek. Like everyone else, I read expressions, and, at times, I sense thoughts or emotions. Perhaps a little better than most people." The smile she offered him somehow made her statement almost intimate. "But I don't read minds, cards or the bumps on your head if you have any. That's strictly carnival stuff. The business the people in this agency and I are in is a very serious one, and I for one can't think of anything more worthwhile than recovering children wrongfully separated from their families.''

He believed her. As long as he looked into her eyes. Striving to hold on to reason, he looked somewhere else. ''Very altruistic.''

Because he was in more pain than he would admit or perhaps even realized, she gave him a great deal of leeway and took no offense at his tone. She knew it was the skeptic in him.

''I'll settle for noble.'' It was time to get down to business. ''So, you didn't come to verbally go ten rounds with me, Mr. Banacek. You came because you weren't so sure you didn't believe me anymore.''

The smile came from nowhere. He wasn't even conscious of it until he saw his reflection in the window behind her. ''I thought you said you didn't read minds.''

''I don't.'' He had a nice smile, she thought, but it didn't reach his eyes. And wouldn't, until he found his daughter. ''I was doing my impression of Sherlock Holmes for you. I was deducing.''

''But you did have that dream about Bonnie.''

''I did have that dream about Bonnie,'' she assured him with quiet intensity.

If he were someone else, listening to himself talk, he would call himself a fool. And yet, here he was, grasping at straws. ''And in your dream, she was alive.''

"Very much so." Reaching, Eliza placed her hand on top of his. "She *is* alive, I'm sure of it."

He couldn't believe he was actually asking questions like this. But he was a man who had come face-to-face with his desperation all over again.

"How often are these dreams—?" He stopped, trying to find the right word that wouldn't make him look like some talisman-clutching fool. He was angry at himself for being here, for hoping. But he continued to do both.

"Accurate?" she supplied. She took a breath, wondering how to phrase this to his satisfaction. He hadn't come here wanting to be convinced, he'd come here daring her to convince him. "There's no easy answer for that."

Double-talk. He might have known. Disgust filled him. "I thought so."

"No," she countered, raising her voice ever so slightly as he rose from his seat, "you didn't." He sat down again, his body language telling her that he was ready to walk out in a heartbeat unless she said something to convince him to remain—and said it soon. "Otherwise, you wouldn't have come here, when doing so flies in the face of everything you hold logical. And to get back to your question, it isn't easy to give you a straight answer because my dreams aren't predictions. They're things that somehow, on some level, I sense. At times, they're other people's pasts—at others, their futures."

Belatedly he realized he was holding his breath,

and released it. This wasn't true, none of it. Why was he even listening to her?

Because he wanted her to convince him. Somehow, some way, he wanted her to make him believe there was some connection between her and his daughter. A connection that would lead him to Bonnie.

"Which was this?"

"The past. The recent past," Eliza clarified. "Perhaps even the present."

He could feel his patience wearing thin. "Can't you give me a straight answer?"

She didn't see the anger, she saw the anguish. "This isn't a science. And even if it were, not even science always gives you a straight answer. Just a hypothesis that might or might not be proven, under the right set of conditions."

He'd listened long enough. This time, he rose to his feet and remained there. "Look, if this is all going to be just mumbo jumbo, then I'm wasting my time and you're wasting yours."

As he began to turn away, she called after him in a strong, steady voice that was far more forceful than the one she'd just used. "Fact, I had the dream. Fact, the girl in the dream was your daughter. Fact, I heard her calling out to you."

He turned to her. There was a dangerous look in his eyes, like that of a man who'd been asked to endure too much.

"To me? What did she say?"

She could still hear the voice in her head. "'Daddy, where are you? Come find me. Please!'"

Damn her, she was playing on his emotions, nothing more. He was wrong to have allowed himself to be led by his feelings. He had to get out of here before he lost his temper completely—and before she found a way to sucker him into this.

He was certain she had no difficulty doing that with her marks. She had the look of breeding about her: genteel, but uncommonly attractive. With eyes that could see into a man's soul. But no matter how she dressed herself up, no matter how lovely her features, she was still nothing more than a con artist. She'd probably gotten her training very young, learning how to use her assets to separate people from their money, and play on their hopes and fears.

But he wasn't a player. Not anymore.

"All well and good." He crossed to the door. "And when you have another dream—" he took hold of the doorknob, twisting it "—maybe you can—"

"There's something else."

He didn't bother hiding his contempt. "I rather thought that there would be, but I'm not—"

She sensed this was important to him and said the words very slowly. "She had a bedraggled pink toe shoe with her."

Walker's mind went numb. And then anger washed over him. White, hot anger. "Is this some kind of sick joke?"

She tried not to take offense. "Nothing about kidnapping, or finding a kidnapped child, is a joke, Mr. Banacek.''

His anger had no direction; she was the only target available. "Stop calling me Mr. Banacek—you make me feel like this is a corporate meeting.''

"All right—Walker, then,'' she allowed cautiously, watching his eyes.

He struggled to be reasonable. "How did you know about the toe shoe?''

In all the stories, the police had kept this one fact back, thinking somehow it might be a clue that would allow them to separate the truthful from the frauds who called in, looking for their fifteen minutes of fame.

"I saw it.''

He told himself not to believe. But no one knew about the shoes that had meant so much to Bonnie. "Saw it? Saw it where?''

"It was in the pocket of her overalls. She was wearing a pair of worn overalls that were too large for her. She kept the toe shoe in her pocket to make her feel better, careful to hide it from whomever it was who'd taken her.''

It took effort to keep the wave of emotion in check, to keep it from pounding down on him like a driving rain. Very quietly, he walked back to the chair he'd just vacated and sat down.

Gripping the arms of the chair, he tried to make himself relax, and succeeded only marginally.

"All right, Eliza, you have my attention.''

Chapter 4

There wasn't much of the dream left to tell. She had given Walker the highlights.

What remained was a haze of feelings—oppressed, frightened feelings emanating from the little girl. It was that, more than anything else, that had sent her searching through the myriad faces on the Internet site.

But that was also something the man sitting on the other side of her desk didn't need to hear right now. There was no reason to make him acutely aware that his daughter was afraid. It was a silent given; both knew it to be true, without having to exchange the actual words.

Eliza told him what she could, repeating the description of both the farmhouse and the land surrounding it. She gave him as accurate a picture of Bonnie as she could.

And when she was finished, Eliza could read the question in his eyes. He was afraid that Bonnie had forgotten him. It wasn't uncommon for minds that young to mix reality with fantasy, fact with fiction, until the truth faded away into the misty past. Maybe Bonnie had begun to believe she'd dreamed about having another father, another mother, and had accepted the ones who had her now as her parents.

"She still remembers you," Eliza told him softly. "Still won't accept her situation."

Like an arrow shot straight and true, her words hit his heart dead center. It was as if she'd read his mind. No matter what her claims to perception were, the reality of it startled him. *Had* she read his mind?

"Her situation," he echoed. It was a euphemism that could mean anything, encompass anything. He needed everything spelled out so that somehow, some way, he could find a little bit of peace, grasp on to a little bit of hope. "Can you tell what her 'situation' is?"

She heard the quiet edge in his voice. The storm was coming.

"I don't think they're treating her badly." At this point, she couldn't tell him that with any certainty, and she refused to lie.

Walker's temper erupted again. He was having less and less success keeping it in check. "How can they *not* be treating her badly? They *kidnapped* her."

She wished there were some way to calm him. All she could do was tell him what she knew. "There're many reasons people kidnap children. It's not just for ransom, or for child pornography," she added, reading the unspoken fear that had surfaced in his eyes. "Some children are abducted to fill a void left by either a child who died, or one who was never there to begin with."

He shook his head. It was as if her words were bouncing off him, refusing to sink in. Emotionally frustrated, with no outlet, he felt himself becoming almost dull-witted. "Meaning?"

"People, women predominately, want a baby so badly, they'll do anything to get one." She spoke slowly, measuring out her words. Trying to reach him before he became lost in the place where he'd retreated. "When they can't get pregnant either because of infertility or lack of opportunity, they become obsessed with having a baby. Some women have been known to go through all the stages of pregnancy, right up through the contractions involved in labor, when they're not pregnant to begin with."

He looked at her as if he thought she were making it up. He was a skeptic, through and through, Eliza thought, smiling. She'd encountered more than her share.

"The mind is a very powerful, underused tool. Any scientist will tell you that," she added as she saw him open his mouth to protest. "Whoever took Bonnie wanted a child so badly, when they saw yours, ev-

erything just clicked into place. They had to have her.
Desire, means and opportunity all came together for
one split second, and they grabbed that second and
ran.''

If he was to control his anger, he couldn't think
about that, about someone swooping down and
snatching his little girl away.

"Which would explain why the ransom note never
came.'' He shook his head, remembering. "I was so
certain she was taken for the money. I didn't sleep
for three days, waiting for the kidnapper to call. The
phone rang off the hook,'' Walker added bitterly,
"but it was never the kidnapper. Half the time it was
some reporter wanting to interview us. As if Bonnie
being kidnapped was some kind of diversionary en-
tertainment for the public to watch on the evening
news.''

She understood where he was coming from. She'd
had a few run-ins with insensitive reporters herself,
though she'd found others to be tactful and caring,
putting people above stories. "Being on the Fortune
500 list unfortunately makes you a target for all sorts
of things. Invasion of your privacy included. It's only
natural that the first thing you think of is that your
daughter was taken for the money. You might find
this hard to believe, but in a way, it's a good thing
that she wasn't.''

"A good thing? How could it possibly be 'a good
thing'?'' he demanded angrily. "How can having
your daughter kidnapped *ever* be a good thing?''

"Not the kidnapping itself," she corrected gently. "I meant the fact she wasn't taken for ransom." She chose her words carefully, knowing that, his rugged appearance to the contrary, Walker Banacek was in a delicate state. "There are times, too many times, when the child is not returned in exchange for the ransom money. The money's taken and the child is never seen again."

He looked at her, stealing himself off from her words, his expression stoic. "Because they've been done away with."

She accepted the euphemism, understanding Walker needed to use it in order to keep the horror at bay. "Because they've been done away with," she echoed. "Whoever took Bonnie from that parking lot wanted to have a child to love. That will keep her safe."

Usually, she added silently.

That was something else Walker didn't need to be made aware of: the fact that there were no hard-and-fast rules to this, only generalities that formed patterns.

Eliza couldn't help wondering how the man in her office would react if he knew she was acting as his protector, keeping things from him she sensed might be too devastating for him to deal with. Probably not well at all, despite the good intentions behind it, she concluded. Walker Banacek didn't strike her as a man who took kindly to being kept in the dark.

"You said 'they,'" Walker began, then hesitated.

He couldn't believe he was asking this. Moreover, he couldn't believe that he was actually ready to believe whatever her answer might be. But Eliza had somehow known about the toe shoes, and no one but the FBI had been given that piece of information. That did make her claim more credible.

"Did you see how many of them there were? In your dream?" he added, feeling foolish and agitated at the same time.

Eliza continued watching his expression, knowing that the answer she gave wasn't what he wanted to hear. "I didn't see anyone else."

He could feel his frustration beginning to build again. "But then, how do you know it's not just a man or a woman involved?"

"I sensed them, their presence," she clarified before he could say anything. "They were close by, looking for her."

"Looking for her?" He didn't understand. Part of him still felt this woman was just toying with him, seeing how far she could lead him down the garden path before he yelled, *"Enough!"* "Why? Where was she? Did she run away from them?"

Eliza shook her head. She knew how all this had to sound to him and she wished she could give him more concrete answers, but she wasn't about to make up anything. One fabrication, one stretch of the truth, and any trust she might be able to build up in him would be irrevocably shattered.

"I'm not sure. Maybe she was just playing in the field and had gotten separated from them."

It made sense, he supposed. But with the logic came a numbing realization. It felt as if something had died within him.

"Then it was someone else she was calling 'Daddy,'" he concluded bitterly.

"No—"

The firm note in her voice surprised him.

"It was you she was calling to."

He couldn't tell if Eliza was just saying what she knew he wanted to hear. "How could you tell?"

"I just knew," she told him simply. "I could feel what she was feeling."

He couldn't allow himself to get strung out on false hopes. Though it cost him, Walker tried to approach this as logically as he could. "Couldn't you have just gotten confused—dreamt about the actual search that went on at the time of her kidnapping?"

The background had been hazy, but not the feelings she'd experienced. "No, these were the people who had kidnapped her. They were looking for her. A man and a woman."

"A man and a woman," he repeated. All right, if he was buying into this, he was going to go all the way and pretend she was telling him something that was real. "What did they look like? Can you describe them?"

If it were only that easy. But at times, her gift just frustrated her, teasing her with pieces of a puzzle that refused to take its true shape. "I wish I could, but as I told you, I didn't actually see them."

"You didn't actually 'see' her, either," he said pointedly. The disdain in his voice was aimed more at himself than at her.

It was going to be a struggle for him to come around. But she already knew that. "Not in the sense you mean, no."

He didn't want to be patronized. His eyes narrowed. "Not in any sense."

This wasn't getting them anywhere. "If you want to help me find your daughter, Mr. Banacek, you're going to have to stop challenging me at every turn, and accept some things on faith."

He laughed shortly. "Faith is something that I find in very short supply right now. And it's Walker, not Mr. Banacek," he reminded her.

He realized that he'd snapped the last part at her, and took a breath to calm himself. He was coming at her like an angry timber wolf emerging from a gutted forest, and that wasn't helping matters.

Walker tried again, his voice lower this time. "What did you mean just now, when you said if I wanted to help you find my daughter?"

She folded her hands before her, her gaze locking with his. She couldn't make it any plainer than she had. "Just what I said."

"What you said made it sound as if you intended to look for her whether or not I hired you." That couldn't be right.

To his surprise, she nodded. "That's about the size of it."

No one did something for nothing. There was always an angle being played. He'd learned that the hard way, and until he'd learned it, he'd never gotten ahead. "Why? Why would you do that?"

Her eyes never wavered. "Because I have to. It's as simple as that."

It wasn't as simple as that, not really, she thought. But he wouldn't understand her reasons. They weren't practical enough for someone like him. She felt compelled to find the girl who'd reached out to her so piteously. Somehow, Bonnie's spirit had connected with hers, and Eliza knew that if she ignored that, ignored the cry for help, she was as guilty as the people who'd taken the child in the first place. She couldn't live with herself if she didn't help Bonnie.

Walker continued looking at the woman before him in silent wonder. She'd moved him. Against all logic—and he prided himself on being a logical thinker, perhaps at times too logical—Eliza Eldridge had managed to move him. More than that, he believed her. Believed that *she* believed what she was telling him. As skeptical as he was about this whole process of clairvoyance and its accompanying mumbo jumbo, he found himself believing in this petite, determined young woman who'd shaken him down to his very foundation.

Faith, huh? She wanted him to have faith. Well, maybe he would give it one more try—even though it was a little like crossing a chasm on a bridge made of whipped cream, he thought, mocking himself.

Very slowly, Walker nodded. "All right, if you're going to do it, anyway, then I might as well pay you for your time."

She smiled at the way he put it. "Cade will be happy to hear that."

Cade Townsend. The man who founded the agency, Walker recalled. Just what manner of people were the members of this organization that had found its way into his life? "But he would have let you undertake this investigation even if I didn't? Or did you intend to look for Bonnie on your own time?"

He was being won over, Eliza could see it. Feel it. "Both. Whenever any of us are on a case, there is no 'own time.' Every waking moment is devoted to the case. And yes, Cade would let me undertake the investigation even if you didn't hire ChildFinders."

That made no sense to him. It just wasn't practical. And yet, it gave him immense comfort. "That must be some boss you have."

"He is." There was pride in Eliza's voice. She'd never felt as close to any person before—aside from her great-aunt—as she did to the people she worked with. "But Cade prefers to think of himself as just a partner, not a boss. We're all partners in the firm from the moment we join," she explained. She had no idea just how well he'd had ChildFinders investigated, but there was something he needed to know. Something that he would find encouraging. "Five of us have experienced kidnappings firsthand. That's part of what makes the agency so dedicated and so effective.''

''Five?''

She nodded. ''Cade began the agency when his son, Darin, was kidnapped. Megan Wichita and Rusty Andreini are brother and sister. Their brother Chad was abducted from in front of their house when he was eight. He's part of the agency, too.''

''That's four.'' His eyes narrowed. ''Are you the fifth?''

She knew he'd probably be comforted if she said yes. She knew that to his way of thinking, that would give her a more personal insight. But she had to disappoint him. ''No, Savannah Walters is. She came to the agency when her daughter was kidnapped in the middle of a crowded department store. Sam was the one who found her. They were married shortly thereafter,'' she added with a smile.

Five. The number astounded Walker. ''Maybe I am in the right place, then.''

Eliza smiled at that. But she knew he couldn't be pushed. He had to proceed at a pace that he set himself. ''Maybe you are.''

Walker shifted in his seat, bracing as he opened himself up to the business of reliving the most anguish-laden days of his life. ''All right, what do you need to know?''

She wanted to spare him as much as possible. ''I'm already aware of most of the details of the actual kidnapping.'' To support her statement, in case he thought she had somehow divined the details, she indicated the open files that littered her desk.

Curious, Walker turned one of the files around to face him so that he could glance through it. Though he'd accepted the fact that she was on the level about deciding to work on the case, he couldn't help being impressed by the preliminary data she'd gathered.

Finished, he turned the folder back around. "You weren't kidding about taking on the case on your own."

"No, I wasn't kidding." She needed to get the unspoken words that existed between them out of the way so they could proceed. The part about his wife. She made her way through the minefield cautiously. "I know how Bonnie was taken from the parking lot of a grocery store in the middle of the day, and how every lead the FBI followed turned out to be a dead end."

He knew where she was going with this. "And that my wife committed suicide two months later because she couldn't live with the grief and the guilt." That, too, had made the newspapers.

Sympathy infused every syllable Eliza uttered. "She had nothing to feel guilty about."

According to the reports she'd read, Rachel Banacek had only turned away from her daughter for less than half a minute to load the nonperishable groceries into the back seat of the van. The van's rear door was open, blocking her view of Bonnie, who was sitting in the shopping cart's child seat. It was the kind of thing that happened countless times throughout the country every day—careless acts by women who were otherwise excellent, caring mothers. No one watching Rachel would have thought anything of it.

Except that this time, there was someone watching her. Someone who took the opportunity to quickly snatch the little girl out of her seat and whisk her away in a car before Rachel was even aware that anything had happened.

Walker could feel his heart constrict within his chest as he thought of his late wife. He'd found her in bed when he'd come home from working late, an empty bottle of sleeping pills standing beside a glass holding the remnants of a gin and tonic. She'd left a note addressed to him with two words on it: *I'm sorry.*

"Rachel didn't see it your way," he said. Because she could easily read the feeling evident in his eyes, Walker looked away. "And maybe I'm to blame for that." He had no idea why he was telling her this. He'd kept it bottled up inside for so long. But now it felt as if his chest would explode if he kept it in a moment longer. "As the days go by after a child's stolen from you, you start looking for reasons, start pointing fingers at each other because you can't deal with the pain you're feeling. Rachel was in a fragile state of mind. I knew that. Her doctor even called me at the office to tell me." There were days when he felt as if the guilt would tear him apart. That's how he knew how Rachel had to have felt at the end. "I wasn't as much of a comfort to her as I could have been."

They'd gone off into their separate corners, to nurse wounds that refused to heal. Rachel had blamed him for never being around when she needed him, leaving her to run their home and raise Bonnie on her own, for the most part. He'd blamed her for being careless. For losing Bonnie. It had come to a head one morning when he'd found her drinking before first light.

It was the last time he ever saw her alive.

"Your wife blamed herself for the kidnapping."

He looked at her, his eyes cold. He'd said too much to this stranger. "Is that a guess, or do you just 'know'?"

He was being hostile again, she thought. "It's a safe assumption. Just as it's a safe assumption that you blame yourself for your wife's suicide." Her eyes were kind. "Don't."

The last thing he wanted was someone's pity. "Just like that, huh?" It wasn't easy keeping the bitterness out of his voice.

"It's a first step. No one makes us do things we don't give them permission to. Your wife lost hope. She wasn't as strong as you."

That was where she was wrong. He found it oddly comforting that she didn't know everything.

"I sure as hell don't feel very strong now." Impatient to get on with it, he raked his hand through his hair. "Look, can we dispense with the emotion and just concentrate on the facts?"

He was uncomfortable with his emotions, she thought. Was that because he didn't think a man should display them, or because he couldn't handle what he was experiencing? "You're going to have to accept that on some level they're inseparable."

He damn well didn't have to accept anything of the kind. "I'd like to operate on the level where they're not for a while, okay?"

It would come. In time, it would come. For now, she let it drop. "Okay."

He wasn't fooled. She'd agreed too easily. But he was so glad to change the direction of the conversation, he didn't care if her retreat was sincere. "All right, what do you need from me?"

That could be summed up in one all-encompassing word. "Cooperation."

"Done. And in return—"

This part was easy, Eliza thought, anticipating his words. He wasn't the first to make the request. Several of the investigators had found themselves unexpectedly partnered with the clients they were working for. The need to be active in the search for a loved one was a common one.

"You want to take part in the search, be there every step of the way." He was staring at her uneasily, she noted, amused. "Go where I go, know what I know."

Maybe there really was something to this clairvoyance nonsense at that. Or maybe he was more of an open book than he'd ever thought. "Is that another one of your safe assumptions?"

A little mystery was a good thing, she thought. Eliza smiled at him. "Are you going to keep questioning me about everything?"

He had a need to make sense of things, even when no sense was evident. "From where I'm standing, you're the one with all the answers."

It made her laugh softly. Nothing could be further from the truth. At times, she felt as if she was more in the dark than anyone.

"Not all," she assured him.

Walker was struck by the honesty he saw in her eyes. Hope, small, unformed, like wisps of smoke, vaguely stirred within him. "The only thing I care about is the important one."

She slipped her hand over his, making a silent pact. "So do I."

Chapter 5

"Why do we have to move for?" Despite her girth, the heavyset woman cowered before the tall, slight man when he looked at her sharply in response to her question, his dark eyes narrowing to slits. "I like it here."

"You liked it in the place we were before, too." Fingers permanently blackened from axle grease wrapped around the stub of a cigarette hanging from his thin lips, and removed it. The man flicked the butt onto the dingy vinyl flooring, then crushed it beneath his boot. "You'll like it in the next place."

His tone warned her not to pursue the subject.

Deaf to the warning, the woman threaded nervous fingers through her dirty, stringy hair.

"But I don't see why we have to," she whined.

She looked around the tiny apartment. It had come furnished with someone else's castoffs, but she had tried to make it a home for the three of them. "I just got all my pretty things laid out the way I like them." Her face fell into a mournful expression. "Can't we please stay this time?"

The edge in his voice became dangerous. "And live on what?"

She read the look in his eyes. The look she knew so well. Defeat seeped into her large bosom. "You lost your job again?"

He kicked over a chair, and it came crashing to the floor. The spark of fear that leaped into her eyes pacified him somewhat.

"Hey, don't make it sound like it's my fault. It ain't. It's just bad luck. Bad luck," he reiterated. Like tiny black marbles, his eyes rolled over toward the child sitting in the corner. The little girl appeared to be playing with imaginary playmates, oblivious to the sound of arguing voices around her. His expression deepened into stark ugliness. "Bad luck ever since she came into our lives."

Suddenly terrified of the words that were hovering in the air about to be spoken, words she'd heard before, the woman jumped up from the small, wobbly table.

"Well, if we're moving, I'd better get started packing," she announced quickly, her voice breathless. "How long do we have?"

Placated, he fished a half-empty pack of cigarettes

from his shirt pocket and coaxed out a single slender cylinder. ''I got another job at a garage in Reno. It starts tomorrow.''

''Reno?''

''Yeah, Reno. You got a problem with that?''

''No.'' The answer was automatic, wrapped in self-preservation.

Tomorrow, she thought numbly. She looked around the shabby room. Very little of this was theirs. Still, it took time to put the things that did belong to them into the suitcases and boxes she would need. ''Does it have to be tomorrow?''

''Yeah, it does,'' he barked at her. ''And you better hurry, woman.'' He crossed to the front door. It was close to sunset, time a man started drinking. ''Unless you want to pay the consequences.''

Without a word, she turned on her worn slippers and scurried into the bedroom.

The front door slammed, reverberating throughout the small apartment.

The room was emptied of adults.

The child in the corner drew herself up, making herself as small as she could be, afraid the man might come back and take his anger out on her. She shut her eyes tight.

Soon. Find me soon. Please, Daddy, find me soon.

Are you all right?''

Walker's question came to her from a great distance. Eliza blinked, realizing that, in layman's language, she had temporarily zoned out. It took effort to force back the chill she felt around her heart. "Yes, sorry."

The woman had all but gone into a trance, Walker thought. He had to admit that it had been unsettling to watch her face suddenly lose all expression, as if some giant eraser had been passed over it.

"Was that for my benefit?"

Eliza tried to orient herself. It always took a moment after one of these episodes. Like a homecoming after a long trip, the last of which was undertaken blindfolded. Answering questions didn't help the process. "Excuse me?"

He tried to put it into words, to make sense out of something that he vaguely felt might ultimately defy explanation.

"That distant stare you just had on your face. Like you were suddenly a million miles away. If you were a student in a classroom, I would have said you were daydreaming." That was it, he told himself, just something she'd done just for effect. Still... "But you're supposed to be a clairvoyant, so I thought that maybe..." His voice trailed off.

"I was giving you your money's worth?" Eliza guessed at the unspoken part of his thought. Her smile was soft. Time had taught her tolerance. Far more tolerance than he was exhibiting. "Number one, I'm not 'supposed to be a clairvoyant.' Unfortunately, I am one. Number two, there is no need to 'impress' you since you are not a believer, but highly skeptical of me, and it would take far more than just a 'day-dreaming stare' to change your mind. And three, I don't need to pretend to do that—it happens enough on its own.''

And there were many times she wished she could turn these visions that burst upon her unannounced off and on like a spigot.

One thing she said caught Walker's attention more than the rest. ''Why 'unfortunately'? You said you are a clairvoyant 'unfortunately,''' he repeated. ''I'd think that if this kind of ability were actually possible, it would be a fortunate thing, not an unfortunate one.''

Did he really not believe she was what she said she was, or was he still challenging her to convince him? she wondered.

''Maybe I can put it into terms that make sense to you.'' She thought for a second. ''It's like having a television set on twenty-four hours a day when you only have intermittent cable service. You just never know when something is going to come on or what it might be. I can't 'summon,' I can't 'channel,' I can't choose. Usually, whatever I see 'chooses' me.'' It was the best way she could describe the gift she had. It controlled her; she didn't control it.

She was telling him not to get his hopes up, he thought. ''So, being this thing—this clairvoyant—it doesn't help you as an investigator at all.''

He was giving up before they began. She had her work cut out for her, Eliza thought.

"I didn't say that. There are things I can do that sometimes help stimulate my 'seeing' something." Pausing, Eliza looked into his eyes. There was no need to wish she could read minds; his thoughts were easy to read. "You're not comfortable with any of this, are you?"

Walker laughed sharply, wondering himself a fool. "Not in the least."

This was nothing new to her. But he had come seeking her out. More than that, he'd hired her and the agency she represented. Was he rescinding that now? "So why *are* you here?"

Because the desperate man he'd been two years ago was not dead, only hidden, and that man had surfaced again. "Because I can't leave any stone unturned. Because if there's a chance, the slightest chance, that you're even remotely on the level, I have to try. To try to find Bonnie." *If she's alive,* he added silently. "I don't have anything to lose." He fixed her with a penetrating look—as if to divine the lie from her, if there was a lie. "You had to know about the toe shoes somehow."

"Yes, I did," Eliza agreed. "I saw Bonnie holding one. To be completely honest, I *felt* her holding it. Holding her hand over it while it was tucked behind the bib of her overalls and against her heart."

He wasn't going to let this get to him, he promised himself, even as he felt his eyes sting. "She always wore them."

Eliza wasn't sure if he was trying to point out a

flaw in her story, or sharing information. "She was four when she was kidnapped. Now she's six. Feet grow fast at that age."

His heart was seized in a vise grip. How many never-to-be-regained milestones had he missed in his daughter's life?

Looking away, he shoved his hands into his pockets. "Yeah. A lot of changes happen at that age."

There was a sadness in his voice that threaded its way into her heart. She felt compelled to comfort him. "We'll find her."

He looked at her sharply, remembering another so-called "seer" saying the same words to his wife. When those words turned out to be empty and Rachel couldn't take it anymore, she had killed herself.

"Don't make promises you can't keep, Ms. Eldridge."

He was being formal again. Whatever line they'd crossed earlier had been re-crossed for some reason. But they weren't back where they'd started, she was willing to bet money on that.

"I don't," she answered quietly. "Now, I need you to take me back to your house."

He stiffened immediately. "Why?"

"I need to see her room, touch her things." And he didn't want her to, she thought, reading his expression. "That's what I meant by saying that sometimes things help stimulate the process. Touching certain objects that were close to the person at times allows me to get a sense of what's happening."

His expression grew only more skeptical, even though he wanted to be convinced, wanted her to say something that would take him from his side of the fence and place him not on it, but squarely on her side of it. "But not always."

"No." This wouldn't work unless she was being completely honest with him at all times. "Not always. We can only try and see—and hope." She saw the look in his eyes, the hesitation in his bearing. "Is that a problem for you?"

"No, not a problem. But it might take a little while. Bonnie's things are packed up and put away." He didn't owe the woman an explanation, but he heard himself giving one, anyway. "After—after my wife died, I couldn't handle having all those reminders around."

"So you packed them up and put them in the attic." As she said it, in her mind's eye, Eliza could see him doing it, climbing the stairs with box after box. Sealing his heart away.

He couldn't read her expression or her tone, but he projected his own feelings. "I suppose you think that's callous."

Her smile was meant to put him at ease, with himself if not with her. "On the contrary, I think that's very sensible. You did what you needed to do in order to survive. You were trying to move on with your life. That's a positive action."

He knew some who didn't think so. His sister had

been appalled that he could just put Bonnie's things out of his life like that.

"What if she's found?" Patrice had asked. *"How's she going to feel, thinking that her father gave up and thought her dead?"*

It was something he would handle when the time came. *If* the time came.

"Are you always this optimistic in your outlook?" he asked her.

She liked the glimmer of a smile she saw on his lips. If a person could smile, hope was not as alien a commodity as it was first thought to be. "Whenever possible."

He didn't understand eternal optimism. Especially if she was the clairvoyant she claimed to be. Didn't seeing into the future mean seeing the dark side of what was to come? "Hasn't anyone ever shot you down?"

If she only had a dime for each time, she thought. "They've tried, Walker. They've surely tried."

"But never succeeded." By her expression, he could see he was right.

She spread her hands wide, as if that were enough to drive the point home. "I'm still here."

He didn't know if that was a lucky thing or not. At least, as far as he was concerned.

Despite the fact that there was still several hours before evening, Walker switched on the light as they entered the attic. Precious little sunlight managed to work its way into the space.

The attic ran the length of the second floor. Most of it was empty. But there were stacks of boxes in two of the corners. Stacks of possessions. Stacks of memories.

He watched as dust motes swirled around, seeming to dance in the light. "It's all dusty. I could have someone—"

But she held up her hand to stop him. There was no need to move anything for her benefit, and it would only bother him. "Dusty doesn't matter. There's dust everywhere." She gestured vaguely, taking in the world at large. "It doesn't bother me."

This time when he laughed, there was humor in the tilt of his mouth. "Too bad my mother didn't meet you before she died."

Crossing to the stack farthest from the door, Eliza turned around to look at him. Her eyes met his.

A scene streaked through her mind, as clearly as if it were a small film clip from his life. A woman with a kindly face, on her knees, scrubbing a kitchen floor that didn't need it.

Eliza could relate to that. "I clean when I'm restless or nervous, too."

Walker's mouth dropped open. That was a piece of information no amount of looking into and examining his life would have unearthed. To know Sylvia Banacek's habits was to have known Sylvia. But his mother had passed on over ten years ago.

"How did you—?"

She gave him a simplified explanation. "I saw it in your eyes."

If that was true… "You scare men away, don't you?"

He'd struck a nerve, but it was one she'd learned how to deal with. "Sometimes." She shrugged the admission away. "I try not to."

That bothered her, he thought, having people shy away from her. For the first time, he began to think of her as a woman rather than as someone with a service to offer that might or might not be legitimate. "A man doesn't like having his thoughts read."

Tell me something I don't know. She kept the reply to herself. Instead, she gave him fact. "I don't do that in the traditional sense."

Men in his experience didn't split hairs. The very thought of a woman being able to actually see through them would send most of the ones he knew running for the hills. Was she lonely? he wondered, then told himself that had no bearing on anything. "But close enough to make an impression."

"At times," she allowed. "When I really make contact with someone." The way she was right now, she added silently. Because, for a moment, when their eyes had met, their souls had, as well. That was why she'd seen into him as well as she had.

He rolled the words over in his mind. "That would be the ironic part, I suppose."

"Yes, it would," she allowed. It was time to back

away from the personal and get back to why she was here. To discover something about the child who had reached out to her for help.

Drawn by instinct, Eliza made her way over to the corner of the attic where Bonnie's things had been placed. Each one of the boxes had been brand new when packed, its contents clearly labeled on the side. The printing was Walker's. She perceived the image of him standing on the side of the room, writing.

"You're very neat," she commented, looking from one box to another. "You get that from your mother."

She was positively spooky. "Is that a question or a statement?" he asked.

"An assumption." She smiled at him over her shoulder. "Based on previous information."

He realized he was standing too close to her, and took a step back. It didn't seem to help. Maybe it was being in the attic that was doing it. Hands in his pockets, Walker cleared his throat. "I can bring it all down for you if it makes it easier."

Selecting a box, she tore away the tape from the top. It came off in one piece. "It wouldn't make it easier on me, and it would make it harder on you." The silence behind her told Eliza she needed to qualify her words. "Otherwise, you wouldn't have brought her things up here to begin with." He would have continued to coexist with them downstairs. Only having them boxed and put away made it possible for him to go ahead with his life.

He was still not saying anything. Eliza turned to look at him. "Why don't you just leave me up here for a little while?"

He heard the kindness in her voice and it rankled him, though he knew it shouldn't. But he'd never been able to take pity.

Walker forced himself to be reasonable. She was only trying to be nice.

"Seeing Bonnie's things won't bother me." The denial came out far more tersely than he'd intended it to.

She didn't have to be clairvoyant to know otherwise, but she saw no point in contradicting him. "But this might take me a while."

That hadn't occurred to him. He'd just assumed that she would get whatever vibrations—if that was how it was done—from the first object she touched. Still, to leave would be cowardly.

"I've delegated my responsibilities at work for today. There's no place I have to be." *For the first time in a long time,* he thought. It took hope for Bonnie's recovery for him to finally take some time off. How strange was that? he wondered. While Bonnie had been a part of his life, much as he'd loved her, he'd always been too busy at the office to take any time off.

Eliza was losing time, and something made her feel that time was a very important element in all this. She just hadn't worked out how. "Suit yourself."

It wasn't that she minded him watching her—even

if his eyes did feel warmer, more penetrating than most of the eyes that had scrutinized her. She'd been observed before. Closely. It was just that she minded being observed if she came up with nothing. It was quite possible that touching Bonnie's things might not give Eliza any insight, might not give her so much as a minuscule lead as to Bonnie's whereabouts. The guilt associated with that would be tremendous.

There was no reason to feel that way, Eliza admonished herself. She wasn't a preprogrammed robot. She was doing the best she could; no one else could ask more of her than that.

Wrong. She could ask more of herself than that. She *did* ask more of herself. She had always been more critical of her abilities and talents, and their absences at crucial moments, than anyone else.

Very carefully, she opened first one box, then another. The first contained toys, the second clothes. As Walker stood behind her, Eliza carefully laid them all out and then slowly handled each individually and at length. Hoping.

She could feel his eyes on her, watching every movement. At times, there wasn't even the sound of his breathing—only hers. That, and the distant, rhythmic sound of life moving on somewhere beyond the house.

Eliza touched one thing after another with no success.

And then, out of the third box, she took a battered stuffed elephant. One ear was hanging by a tangled thread, clearly having been sewn on several times in the past, and the trunk gave every indication that the misshapen pachyderm was well on its way to a badly needed rhinoplasty.

Holding the toy, she suddenly began to see. The wire mesh of the shopping cart, a pair of hands coming at her. Hands that were pulling her roughly out of the child's seat, covering her mouth to keep her from crying out.

There was the smell of sickeningly sweet perfume. She was inside something. A car. Cracked plastic, discolored with grit and sweat, gray tufts of batting sticking haphazardly out of the seat she was thrown on.

"She's come back, our baby's come back. Drive, drive, drive!"

And then the swirls of light receded, melding with the dim interior of the attic. The images vanished, deserting her.

Eliza stared down at the stuffed animal in her hands, trying very hard to catch her breath. "Bonnie had this with her the day she was kidnapped, didn't she?"

She could have read that in a newspaper account, Walker told himself. Still, his heart jumped at the sound of certainty in Eliza's voice.

"Yes. It was her favorite."

Eliza nodded. She knew that, could feel it the instant she touched the stuffed animal. "She still misses it," she whispered, continuing to stare at the toy. "A woman took her. She called Bonnie her baby and told whoever was driving the car that their baby had come back.''

Suddenly, she felt Walker grab her roughly by the shoulders. The intensity she saw in his eyes stole her words from her.

''You had better be on the level,'' he warned her, fighting to keep his emotions under control. ''Whatever you tell me, you had better be on the level. I can't go through this kind of thing again.''

She felt things then. Things she could identify and things that eluded her comprehension, but were nonetheless there, powerful. Overwhelming. His feelings became hers, and she understood every inch of the anguish-filled road Walker had traveled, only to find one dead end after another.

''I'd never lie to you,'' she told him quietly.

Suddenly aware that he was holding on to her shoulders and that his grip had to be hurting her, he released Eliza. ''I'm sorry.''

''No need.'' There was going to be some bruising there tomorrow, she thought wryly. ''You've been through a great deal. I wouldn't be telling you I could help if I felt I couldn't.''

He merely nodded. Maybe it was better if he left her alone to do this. It was clearly taking too much out of him. ''I'll be downstairs if you need me.''

Without waiting for her response, he withdrew and closed the attic door behind him.

Chapter 6

"I'd like to see her room now, please."

Coming from behind him, the soft voice startled Walker. He saw her reflection in the window he was looking through and realized Eliza must have entered the living room without making a sound.

Maybe she was an apparition herself, he thought. Someone he'd dreamed up in his unconscious desperation to find Bonnie.

But he didn't dream, he reminded himself. Not anymore. Now he just fell into a dark, empty sleep, waking up just in time to get ready to go to work. His life had become all about work now, with little time for anything else. As he saw it, there was no point to anything else, and his recently acquired philosophy concerned his sister and the few people who had the tenacity to hang on and remain his friends.

"Sorry, I didn't hear you come in."

He'd been looking at the breeze move the swing hanging from the tree, the swing he'd put up when Bonnie had begged him to. He'd done it, but only after she'd promised that he had to be the one who pushed her. It had been his way of protecting the little girl.

As the swing moved now, he could almost see Bonnie on it, laughing, begging him to push her "higher, Daddy, higher!"

Turning away from the window, he looked at Eliza. "What did you just say?"

She'd interrupted something, she thought. "That I'd like to see Bonnie's room, and if you have any videos of her, I'd like to see those, too. Anything of that nature would be helpful."

"What does all this have to do with her kidnapping? She was kidnapped, she wasn't a runaway."

She saw impatience creasing his brow. How many times had he smiled in the last two years? she wondered. Probably not very often. "I'm trying to get a feeling for the kind of person she was."

The kind of person she was. He didn't think of Bonnie in those terms. As a "person." She was a little girl and his daughter. Sunshine in pink toe shoes and pink overalls. Energy, laughter, but not a person. It was a word he associated with someone who was beyond the age of twelve. "How does that help find her?"

Eliza had the sudden, strong urge to smooth out the

crease between his eyes. To touch his soul and make it better.

Giving yourself too much credit, Lizzie, she mused. "It helps me make a connection."

He was still trying very hard to find his way through this new maze he found himself in, using the only tool he had: logic. "A connection between facts?"

She shook her head. "A connection to Bonnie."

Like someone from a psychic hot line, he thought in disgust, annoyed with Eliza, and with himself for actually holding on to the hope that this was real.

He waved an impatient hand at her. "I'm sorry, this is just too weird for me."

She wasn't put off. "It is for a lot of people." Eliza followed him as he walked out of the room. "Think of me as an overzealous FBI profiler, if it helps any." That struck a cord. He stopped walking and looked at her.

Her eyes met his. "I need to find Bonnie as much as you do."

He sincerely doubted that. But something inside Walker wanted to give her the opportunity to convince him. "Why?"

The answer was simple. "Because she asked me to. In my dream, she was calling out to you, but the message came to me. I'm not going to be able to sleep until I find her."

She sounded sincere enough about it, he thought. And if he looked into her eyes, he found himself believing. Believing in all sorts of things. In small, petite women who made outlandish promises no one in their right mind would buy into. The power of dreams and visions and things that couldn't be explained by anyone employing a rational thought process.

Desperation, he concluded, had pushed him to the edge of the ledge. "All right, this way."

Walker brought her to a sun-drenched room; on a wall were tiny ballerinas all in a row, executing the five basic ballet positions, their small hands resting delicately on a ballet bar on the wall. The pattern was repeated on the opposite wall.

When she drew closer, Eliza realized that the walls weren't covered with wallpaper, but murals. Someone had spent countless hours doing this. A woman with blond hair and paint smudged on her face flittered through her mind's eye. "Someone was very talented."

Yes, she had been, he thought, blocking out the sadness. "My wife," Walker muttered in reply. The half shrug was almost self-conscious. "When I met her, she told me she liked to paint. I thought she meant rooms." The very slightest hint of a smile came, self-depreciating at its birth. "I guess, in a way I was right."

Up close, Eliza inspected the detail. As she did so, she perceived the image of a little girl giving instructions, clapping her hands. *Bonnie.* "This is beautiful."

He didn't like talking about anything that had to

do with Rachel. It hurt too much for too many reasons.

"Bonnie liked it." It was an understatement. Bonnie had been thrilled by Rachel's efforts. If he tried, he could still hear the girl's squeals of pleasure.

When he'd packed up everything else, he'd been tempted to have someone come in and paint over the walls. But he couldn't make himself do it. He knew if he did, it would be as if the final link to his past were blotted out with the last stroke of the brush. That stroke would take away not only his daughter, but his wife, as well. Maybe it was cowardly of him, but he wasn't prepared for that yet.

"Yes," Eliza murmured, moving around the room slowly. "She did. She liked the room very much."

He'd left the bed, she noticed. Clearly a young girl's bed, with a billowy canopy. It had a white eyelet comforter with matching dust ruffle and pillows. Bonnie had been a female down to her tiny toes. If Walker were as callous as he believed himself to be, this would have been placed into storage, as well.

No matter where she turned, Eliza kept butting up against things that spoke of Walker in one form or another. Now, standing in his daughter's room, she was getting a definite feeling. Not of the missing girl, but of him.

"You were happy here," she said, turning to face him.

He took it to mean that she thought he was happy

in the house itself. His answer was preceded with another careless shrug. "Yeah, maybe."

There was no need to tell Eliza that he and Rachel had begun to drift apart. Drift apart so much that his wife had sought solace in someone else's arms. Rachel had felt so guilty about it, she'd confessed her affair to him, swearing that she would never see the other man again. And that had caused a rift that had never healed. These were things Eliza didn't need to know. They had nothing to do with Bonnie's abduction.

He sought to divert her from any more questions by asking sarcastically, "Is that the house speaking to you now?"

She stopped running her hand along the comforter and looked at him over her shoulder. "Were you always this cynical?"

No, once he'd been a great deal happier, a great deal more open. That, too, was something he didn't want to let her know about, as if in talking about it, he would lose that last little strain forever.

So instead, he looked at her defiantly. "You tell me."

Turning around to face him, Eliza looked intently at him for what felt like a long moment. Walker could feel her eyes delving into him, not invasively like a surgeon's scalpel, but gently, like the first spring breeze when it softly whispers between the leaves of a tree.

"No," she decided, "you weren't. You came here

to live with a great deal of hope, and then something happened.''

This had been his first house. He and Rachel had bought it as newlyweds with the intention of eventually moving on; but somehow, they never did.

Walker held his breath, half expecting Eliza to say something about Rachel's affair. He didn't want to hear the words, didn't want to share with anyone the knowledge, the shame that his wife had betrayed him—and that he had driven her to it.

There was something in his eyes, something she couldn't read, a barrier she couldn't surmount. He had a right to his privacy.

Mentally, Eliza drew back, feeling just the slightest bit shaken. Not because of any secrets that were held in abeyance, but because of the man himself. It was as if his very being was reaching silently out to her. Not bonding, but touching.

She was letting her work get to her. A smile curved her mouth. It was the kind of work she was forced to bring home with her, no matter what. It wouldn't remain ''at the office'' the way other people's work did, because everywhere she went, she was her own ''office.''

Knowing Walker didn't want her to press the issue, Eliza turned away from him and slowly began to move about the room again, touching a curtain, laying her hand on a windowsill, brushing by a window seat cushion. Nothing but a sense of contentment came to her in this room. Bonnie had been happy here. If there was some sort of discord between Bonnie's parents, such as Eliza had sensed from Walker, it never ventured into this room. An invisible barrier kept it out.

Or perhaps a conscious effort by both parents that their daughter was never to be tainted by the sadness that had found them.

Eliza also got a vivid sense of something else. "She was a strong-willed child."

Each time she told him something he knew, he encountered a wave of surprise. "Yes, she was. How did you— I should stop asking that, shouldn't I?"

He was trying to be friendly. It wasn't easy for him. She appreciated the attempt. "You can keep asking if you like, but I really don't have any better answers to give you than the one I already have. It's a feeling I get, being here." It also reflected common knowledge. She turned once in a complete circle, as if absorbing the very air. "It's a bright sunny room for a bright, sunny child. Only children are usually pretty strong-willed because they're accustomed to being the center of their parents' universe."

He'd tried. *Quality time* was such a pitiful term for what he'd wanted to give his daughter. She'd represented the very best part of him, and he had wanted to give her all of himself. But he'd also wanted to give her things, never let her lack for anything—and that took money. Most of all, he'd wanted to give her the peace of security.

"Even if one of the parents is always busy?" he heard himself asking ruefully.

"Even then." Intuition rather than her gift told her things about this man before her. "When you were home, you gave your daughter all your attention, which is what mattered."

"Is it?" He wasn't so sure of that.

But if he had doubts—as she saw in his eyes—she had none. With all her heart, she would have wanted to be in Bonnie's place, to have a tenth of the love, the understanding that child had had. Eliza's father had been closed off to her even before her mother died, and much more so after.

"It was to Bonnie," she told him. "That's why she's calling out to you to come rescue her now."

How did he put this without sounding like some mindless automaton to be led around by the nose? "Look, if I believe you—is she in any danger? Is that why you're getting these visions?"

"Dreams," Eliza corrected.

"Whatever." His impatience with himself and the situation intensified when he saw the slight hesitation on her face. "I have to know the truth—whatever you think it is. I don't want you holding back."

Walker stood back in wonder. Was this really him putting his faith into a soothsayer, a beautiful charlatan—for all he knew—? He'd really reached the end of his rope, hadn't he? he mocked.

She told him as much as she was able, as diplomatically as she could. "I don't know if there's any new danger, but there is this sense of urgency. As if something might change soon if we don't find her."

"Change how?" He bit back an oath, knowing that losing his temper would serve no purpose.

"I don't know." She saw his thoughts in his eyes as plainly as if he'd said them out loud. "Walker—" she spoke to him as if they'd known each other a long time rather than what amounted to a few hours "—these answers I'm giving you are as frustrating for me as they are for you. I don't get clear pictures of things, I get pieces I have to arrange into a whole. I wish it were some other way, but it isn't. I just have to be patient until I can get somewhere."

Patient. Patience was the one commodity he didn't have. It had been lost to him two years ago. "So what do we do now? Where do we go from here? Is watching the videos actually going to be of some help to you?"

There were times when a glimmer of something she saw, something the victim saw as well, hooked up and sparked a vision, a clue. But she wouldn't know that until she watched the tapes.

"They can't hurt."

Yes, he thought, they can. He hadn't looked at any of the videos since the night after the kidnapping, when he'd discovered that viewing a tape of his daughter, laughing and dancing, always dancing, was just too painful to endure. Rachel had walked in on him as he'd sat in the darkened living room, watching the little blond girl giving him his own private dance recital on the front lawn. Bonnie had moved with surprisingly adult-like grace for a child her age. He remembered hearing Rachel start to cry. The sound had echoed the one locked in his heart. He'd put the tapes away after that.

Eliza understood what he left unsaid. "You don't have to watch with me," she told him gently. "But I need to see them."

Somehow, allowing Eliza to view them without him was tantamount to abandoning his child. He couldn't do that, no matter what seeing them would cost him.

"I'll watch them with you."

There was no arguing with his stoic voice.

The picture faded and a blue screen took its place.

That was the last of them, Eliza thought. There had been a total of fourteen tapes in all, tapes involving Christmases and birthdays and "just because," and she'd sat through all of them, watching intently. She could see why someone would be drawn to Bonnie. The little girl lit up the screen even when she had just a corner of it. Everything about her drew attention like a high-powered magnet.

Walker rose from the seat he'd taken beside her, crossed to the VCR. He pressed the rewind button just as he had the other thirteen times. He was surprised to find that he was dry-eyed. He hadn't expected to be.

But there was this lump in his throat that made speaking difficult. "That's the last one."

Eliza shifted, trying to ease the tension from her

body. She'd been keenly alert throughout the entire viewing, waiting for that one moment when something struck her, came to her. But it hadn't. She tried to contain her disappointment, confident in the belief that if one thing did not work, something else would.

"She's a beautiful little girl."

"Yes," Walker agreed, his back to her, "she was."

He was letting despair get to him again, she thought. "Is," Eliza corrected, standing up. Coming up behind him, she placed her hand on his shoulder. "Bonnie's alive, Walker. There's no reason to refer to her in the past tense."

He could feel it, actually feel the despair coming for him like a black, insidious goo. Just as it had the last time, before he'd found a way to put the barricades up. Before he'd found a way to preserve what was left of his sanity.

Angry at being put through all this again, he looked at Eliza sharply. "Damn it, why did you have to come here? Why couldn't you just have rolled over in your bed, gone back to sleep and left me alone?"

"Because I'm going to find her."

How could she be so sure? How the hell could this wisp of a woman be so sure of succeeding where the police and the FBI had failed?

"And if you don't?"

She couldn't believe that the strong vibrations she'd gotten, the clarity and persistent repetition of the dreams, would be for naught.

There was a reason for everything, she'd come to

firmly believe, and she'd had these dreams for only one reason. To find the girl who was calling out in them.

"That's not an option," Eliza informed him quietly but firmly. "I will." She covered his clenched hand with her own. "*We* will."

He felt it then, felt not just her conviction, but the serenity in which she offered it. Her serenity. For just a shred of a second, her peace spoke to him. Filled him. Made him one with her. He felt all her hope and her certainty.

He had to be going crazy.

It would certainly account for what he did next. He had no other plausible explanation as to what possessed him to do it.

Maybe he could have used the excuse that he wasn't in his right mind, but that would have presupposed that he was in his mind at all. And he wasn't. He'd taken complete leave of his senses.

If not, why else, riding on the cusp of a flare of intense emotion, was he suddenly framing Eliza's face with his hands? Why else was he tilting that same face up and kissing her mouth? Hard, as if doing so would give him enough strength to continue, to fill his veins with that strength and give him the energy to follow this quest again, this time to a happy conclusion.

Even under oath he would have had to plead ignorance as to how any of it transpired. But there he was, holding Eliza, lowering his mouth to hers and kissing her. Kissing a woman he didn't know. This, after not having kissed the woman he did know during the last months they'd had left together.

There had been no intimate touching, no kissing, no exchange of endearments or gentler emotions of any sort between him and Rachel for several months before Bonnie's abduction—not since he'd learned of the affair. And there had not been any afterward. The kidnapping had only intensified what had already existed. They'd each gone to their separate corners to grieve, and he had cut Rachel off completely.

The guilt that came in the wake of her suicide was almost too much for him to handle. He'd been forced to bottle it up in order to go on.

Now, the amount of pent-up emotion that poured out astounded him, dragging the very air out of his lungs. Walker felt like a man who had just parachuted from a plane, only to discover that the plane was traveling a great deal higher than he'd first thought and that there was, in actuality, no parachute strapped to his back. As he moved his mouth over hers, there was a feeling of free-falling.

That, and a sense of extreme exhilaration.

She'd seen it coming. Not in any vision, or because some premonition had found her a second before, but in his eyes. Eyes the color of shamrocks at dawn. The second before it happened, he'd looked at her and she'd known what he was going to do. Even if he didn't.

Eliza let it happen, giving herself up to the unexpected rush that found her, the rush that took her prisoner, placing her in the first seat of a plunging roller coaster.

It was a hell of a ride.

There was no thought of being unprofessional, no sudden recoiling at the action. She recognized the kiss for what it was: a veiled cry for help. Walker needed comfort and she needed to give it. More than that, she needed to be the one he was kissing.

She didn't know why yet, but the answer would come.

For the moment, all she could do was to receive and to give. Rising on her toes, letting him pull her to him, she did both. Willingly and gladly.

The consequences would be taken into account and dealt with later. For now, she allowed herself to feel what he was feeling, and made herself one with him.

It had never happened to her quite this way before, and she doubted it would ever happen again.

Chapter 7

Sanity returned.

His complete loss of control appalled Walker. How could he have done such a thing? What the hell was he thinking?

Dropping his hands from Eliza, Walker stepped back, unable to think of what to say to her that could begin to express his sincere apologies.

The words that came out were weak when measured against the feelings involved.

"I'm sorry."

She wasn't and she didn't want him to be. Not for kissing her. Certainly not for needing to make contact with another human being and seeking momentary comfort in that contact. Even now, as her blood was settling back in her veins, she could only call what she'd just experienced one of the more pleasurable events of her life. His kiss had made her forget herself and think only of him. She rather liked that.

Eliza smiled at him, hoping to convey with a look what would probably be too embarrassing to Walker for her to express in words. "Don't be."

Suddenly restless, Walker raked his hand through his hair, moving about the room. "I'm not sure what came over me, I don't usually act that way. I certainly don't give in to—"

Eliza placed her finger to his lips, silencing him. "It's okay, really," she told him quietly. "I understand. This is an emotional situation, and sometimes we channel our emotions in different directions than we're normally accustomed to."

She wanted to touch his cheek, to run her hand along it and soothe him somehow, but she knew that to do so would only agitate him further. So she resorted to what he knew: logic.

"I'm not offended, shocked, harassed or any of the other reactions you think are going through my head," she assured him. The look on his face told him she'd guessed correctly. "You've been through a great deal today, revisiting places in your memory that give you both joy and pain. I shouldn't have let you watch the videos with me." That had been an error in judgment, made in part because she found herself enjoying his company more than she should. She was going to have to watch that. "If you don't mind, I'd like to go through the photo albums alone."

She nodded toward the stack on the coffee table behind her. "I'll take them with me and return them to you tomorrow."

He hated being a coward, and this was cowardly: retreating from looking over Bonnie's photographs. But Eliza was right, it would be better this way. He knew that. Why else had he taken down Bonnie's photographs from around the house?

Still, he didn't like the idea of the albums being out of his possession. Walker gave in with noticeable reluctance. "All right, if you really think it's necessary."

She was determined to be honest with him at all times. Otherwise, when she needed him to trust her, he wouldn't be able to. "At this point, I'm not sure what is necessary—other than finding Bonnie."

He liked the way she kept making that the bottom line. He could feel his hope attaching tiny grappling hooks to things she said, and he prayed that he wouldn't live to regret it.

"Do you want me to come to your office tomorrow? Or will you come here…?" He left the sentence unfinished, letting her complete it.

She thought it would be better all around if they didn't meet at his house again for a little while. It would remind him of his moment of weakness, and that wouldn't do him any good. Until they found Bonnie, their relationship had to remain professional. Afterward…

Afterward, she would probably never see him

again, she surmised. Seeing her might make him uncomfortable. She'd had that happen before, too, and
had made her peace with it.

"The office," she responded. "Nine o'clock, if
you'd like."

He thought an earlier hour might be better, but right
now, he didn't feel like arguing the point. He needed
some time alone.

"I'll be there."

After placing the albums into a large box, Walker
had helped her carry them to her car. There were six
in all. Six large, white albums containing four-and-a-
half years of a life.

It hardly seemed enough, Eliza thought later that
evening as she sat on her bed with the albums spread
out around her like a magic semicircle. She flipped a
few pages of each, going from one to another, trying
to discern why this child had reached out to her. It
was enough that Bonnie had, that the child had been
kidnapped and had somehow managed to contact her
via her dreams—but Eliza wondered if there might be
more.

If there was, she wanted to uncover what that *more*
entailed. Why had Bonnie reached out to her and not
someone else? Why Bonnie and not some other child?

Eliza sighed. Maybe all this mattered and maybe it
didn't. There weren't always answers, and this was
getting to be far too philosophically involved for her.

"What you need is a cup of tea and a nice hot bath," she told herself.

What she really needed was to relax and not allow tension to distort or inhibit anything that might be trying to get through. The visions that came to her were difficult enough to perceive without her getting in her own way, she thought.

Almost involuntarily, her mind turned to Walker, and she felt a smile forming. The man probably thought she was half fraud, half witch.

"Not unlike you, eh, Dad?" she murmured, glancing at one of the framed photographs on her bureau.

There were three in all. One of her and her mother, one of her and her great-aunt, and one of her father by himself. That was the way she remembered him. By himself. Even when he was with her, he really wasn't. He was always removed from her. By choice.

She'd tried so hard to breach that wall he had constructed between them, but he had manned the parapets diligently and she had never been able to find a way to break through. Not even when he was dying.

Her father had called her to his bedside, and in his own way he had attempted to make amends. But the effort, even the words, had been entirely without conviction. He'd summoned her because he'd wanted to die with a clear conscience. But there was still no understanding, no acceptance of who and what she was. With his dying breath, he'd thought of her as an oddity with which he had been cursed.

It hadn't been easy on him.

Or on her.

Suppressing another sigh, Eliza rose from the bed and went to get her tea. She needed something to do other than think.

That night, she dreamed. Not of the little girl—not at first—but of a man with broad shoulders and arms that could break through the barrier that surrounded her, the barrier that separated her from the rest of the world. Dreamed of a mouth that was firm and hard and yet capable of melting her.

He came to her across the sea of time, with no name, no face. A feeling rather than a form.

Yet he was real and her soul knew him.

Slowly, the dream broke up, dissolving in the heat the man generated within her.

And then she saw the child again.

This time, it was clearly Bonnie. Bonnie with her light-green eyes like her father's, staring at her, calling to her, as she ran through the tall grass, now withered and burned by the hot sun. There were tears streaming down her small, sad face, though her eyes remained clear.

Bring my daddy. Make him find me. Hurry!

Eliza heard the words though the child's lips never moved. They echoed in her brain, growing progressively louder until they sounded like a death knell rung from a church steeple.

Gasping for air, Eliza sat bolt upright. Perspiration lined her brow and she shook from the cold. Rubbing the back of her neck, she realized that she'd fallen asleep next to the album she had been poring through.

Her brain fighting its way out of the fog, she reached for her alarm clock—the one she never bothered setting—and read its face. Iridescent blue lights winked flirtatiously at her.

Four-thirty.

Eliza deposited the clock back on the stand. She supposed that four-thirty was as good a time as any to get up.

Sliding off the bed, she moved the albums into a small pile, closing each carefully before going to take her shower.

She couldn't shake the feeling of urgency that surrounded her. It had become part of her since yesterday when it had slipped over her while she was talking to Walker at his house. A tiny burst of a vision she couldn't make sense of yet.

She'd come to the office right after getting dressed, letting herself in with her key. Nursing the cup of coffee she'd brought with her in a lidded travel mug, she'd sat down by her computer and had begun searching the usual Web sites, though deep down inside she had a feeling that none of them would ultimately bear fruit. Not if she were to believe the vision she'd had when she'd held Bonnie's stuffed animal in the attic.

But to be on the safe side, she accessed a Web site listing of registered child molesters in the area. Carefully, she checked out their whereabouts and printed out the results to review later. Of the six known felons at the time of Bonnie's disappearance, three had moved in the past two years, one had violated his parole and was back in prison, and one had recently died. Only one remained in the area.

She supposed that she or one of the others at the agency could go and question the one in prison while tracking down the other three, but deep down she knew it was a dead end. Whoever had taken Bonnie was someone who wanted her. Specifically. Wanted her because she looked like a child they had lost—

"What are you doing here?"

Lost in thought, Eliza looked up to see Savannah Walters peering into the room. She glanced at her watch and saw that it was a little after eight-thirty. She'd been here over three hours.

"Trying to find a needle in a haystack." She rubbed the bridge of her nose, closing her eyes briefly.

Savannah stepped into the room and leaned against Eliza's desk. "What do you need?"

Eliza glanced at the notes she'd made to herself. "Hacking ability, as near as I can figure out."

"Go on—so far you haven't mentioned anything that might not be in my realm of talents."

It wasn't something Savannah would broadcast, nor would she do it for any sort of gain. But if it aided in finding a lost child, she was more than happy to bend the rules a little and access systems that were ordinarily closed to outsiders. Having gone through

the gut-wrenching terror of having her daughter kidnapped, there was nothing that Savannah felt was out
of bounds when it came to recovering a missing child.

Eliza knew she was giving the other woman a tall
order, but if anyone was equal to it, it was Savannah.
"I need you to access hospital records and county
coroner's files. I need to know the names of families
who lost a child two to three years ago. Specifically,
a female child aged three or four."

The number of hospitals in the Southern California
area was staggering. Getting into each of their records
was not going to be an easy feat. "Boy, you don't
ask for much, do you?"

"If it's too difficult—" Eliza began.

"I didn't say it was too difficult," Savannah interrupted before Eliza could go any further. "Granted,
it's not a piece of cake, but give me some time and
I can round up the information for you." Curiosity
highlighted her eyes. "Does this have anything to do
with those dreams you've been having?"

Eliza nodded. "Yes."

"And that man who came to see you yesterday—
is he the father of the child in your dreams?"

Eliza smiled. She liked the way Savannah accepted
all this as if it wasn't anything out of the ordinary.
As if it were normal to dream of kidnapped children
who called out to you. She'd never felt as accepted
as she did here at ChildFinders.

"You'd make a pretty good investigator yourself.
Yes, he's the father of the child in my dreams. His

name is Walker Banacek. His daughter, Bonnie, was kidnapped two years ago from a crowded parking lot.''

''And I'm looking up families who lost their daughters because…?'' Savannah asked.

''I think Bonnie was taken by a woman who was struck by the similarity she saw to her own dead daughter.'' Eliza realized that the smile had left Savannah's face. The other woman looked as if she'd suddenly come face-to-face with a ghost. ''Is anything wrong?''

''*Déjà vu,*'' Savannah replied softly. ''My daughter Aimee was taken by someone who wanted her to replace the daughter she'd lost in a drowning accident. It turned out to be a woman I actually knew.'' Savannah began to back out of the room. ''I'll get right on this,'' she promised.

''Wait—'' Eliza flipped open to the last page of the top album on her desk, then turned it around so that Savannah could see the photograph. ''This might help you. Bonnie looks like this.''

Savannah took the album and looked at the little girl. Her mother's heart melted and constricted with pain at the same time.

''She's beautiful.''

''Exactly,'' Eliza said. And that was what might help them find her. People would remember seeing a little girl this attractive. If Bonnie was even allowed outside. ''Bonnie Banacek would catch anyone's attention. The problem is, she caught the wrong person's attention."

Savannah looked at Eliza. "Why don't I widen that time frame to go back four years instead of three, just to be on the safe side?"

Eliza nodded. "Can't hurt. But it's more work for you," she felt compelled to point out.

Closing the album, Savannah held it against her chest. "It's not work, it's a mission." With that, Savannah walked out.

Mentally, Eliza crossed her fingers.

When Walker came into the office promptly at nine o'clock, he tried very hard not to arrive with raised hopes. After all, the FBI had placed their best people on it and failed. The case still remained open with them, joining so many other open cases. Nothing short of a miracle was going to lead them to Bonnie.

He found himself hoping Eliza was that miracle.

Knocking once on Eliza's office door, Walker entered without waiting to be invited inside. It was difficult bridling his impatience, having finally unleashed it after all this time.

There were papers all over Eliza's desk. He would have thought her to be one of those painfully neat women who had to have everything methodically organized. Showed him what he knew.

"Anything?" he asked.

There were computer printouts everywhere, thanks to Savannah. Lost in her work, trying to feel her way through the myriad names before she undertook the monumental task of seeking out the people on these lists, Eliza hadn't even heard Walker knock.

His face looked more drawn than it had yesterday, she noted. She wondered if he'd gotten any sleep, and then decided that he probably hadn't. He had that slightly haunted look that defined the faces of the parents who came to them with checks and prayers.

Maybe it was unreasonable, but she felt a touch of guilt for doing that to him, for jolting Walker's hopes out of their holding pattern without having anything more substantial to offer him than the recurring dreams that filled her nights.

She half rose in her chair, greeting him, then indicated her desk. "Leads to follow up."

Walker raised a quizzical eyebrow. "Leads, as in sightings, or people to question…?"

He'd run the gamut when they'd gone through this the first time, he and Rachel. It got to the point that he'd had to almost forcibly drag every word out of the mouths of the special agents who were handling his daughter's case. None had been forthcoming about any leads that came in, and there had been many— all going nowhere.

Eliza could feel the frustration he'd gone through. It amazed her how in-tune she seemed to be when it came to Walker.

She told him the news as succinctly as she could. "We have five registered child molesters, four no longer in the area for one reason or another, to question, as well as a great many bereaved families to talk to."

Most, if not all, of whom were going to have their emotions bandied about for the sake of beating the bushes for one person. A person she might not find.

But it had to be done, and she just hoped the parents she would speak to would understand the necessity of questions that might come across like accusations, in order to find one missing child.

Walker picked up several sheets and scanned the page that was on top. "I can understand questioning the molesters." Understood and abhorred the reasons that were behind it. The very thought of needing to talk to these people made his skin crawl. "But why question the bereaved families?"

"Because perhaps one of them sought to ease their grief and somehow mistook Bonnie for the daughter they lost." She saw his jaw tighten to the point that she thought it might snap.

He tossed the list back on the desk. "And you think that person might be in here?"

She caught her lower lip between her teeth. This was the tricky part. "I don't know. If these people's daughter died in another state…"

Eliza left it unsaid. There were already a great many names to sort through. Taking the different states into account would give them an utterly unmanageable number of possibilities.

"All right, let's get started," Walker said.

She looked at him uncertainly. "Let's get started?"

she repeated. Did he intend to come along with her when she spoke to these people? She would have thought that was an awkwardness he'd rather avoid.

"I said I was going to be part of this investigation, and I meant it." He glanced again at the scattered pages. They wouldn't be covered in a day. Perhaps not even in several days. But it was a start. "I want to do whatever it takes to help find my daughter. The last time, when the FBI was handling it, I had to stay on the sidelines. I can't sit on my hands again. I can't go through the waiting. I have to be there, on top of every lead."

She understood his need. She'd never been one to stand on the sidelines herself. Gathering the various pages together, she rose from her chair. "And you won't. Let's go."

And with that, she led the way out the door.

Chapter 8

They'd been at this for almost a week. Six days, to be exact. It felt longer.

There had turned out to be twenty-nine names on the lists that Savannah had compiled from the various hospitals in the Southern California area. Twenty-nine blond girls between the ages of two and four who had died during the time frame they were examining. A preliminary search through various public records and databases had shown up nothing out of the ordinary, other than young lives taken too soon. Freak accidents and illnesses had claimed them; there had been nothing suspicious or noteworthy about any of the deaths, nothing suspicious thereafter.

Eliza had gone to each family on the list, aching each time she rang the doorbell. Aching for the people on the other side of the door, and for the man who doggedly accompanied her on each and every call. It was hard to say which of them suffered more from the interviews, the families or Walker. Eliza could see that he was reliving the first shock of his loss with each stop they made.

Because Walker had been so insistent about being there for every step, Eliza had purposely asked Rusty to look into the child molesters for her. In Walker's current frame of mind, she was afraid of what he might do when confronting one of the five people on the list.

They stopped at a traffic light. Walker was looking worn, Eliza thought, glancing at his profile. They had put in ten hours today, starting early and driving from one place to another, talking to family after family. Walker had asked her, when they'd begun this odyssey six days ago, just what it was she was hoping to find.

"Bonnie," she'd answered simply. "I'm hoping to either see a six-year-old girl pop up unannounced, or get a sense of your daughter on the premises."

And he'd been skeptical and challenging as always. Having gotten to know what to expect, Eliza would have been disappointed if he hadn't been.

"I thought you said you couldn't call these 'things,' whatever they are, up at will."

"I can't," she'd confirmed again. "But those dreams are so strong, all I can think is that it has to mean, however temporarily, that there's a very real bond between Bonnie and me. If she's around, that should mean I can sense it.''

"So in essence, you're a psychic bloodhound."

She'd smiled at the description. ''Not very flattering or poetic, but yes, that about sums it up.''

And me as well, she'd thought. At least in his eyes.

Cynicism gave way to amusement, however minor. ''Never had a conversation with a bloodhound before,'' he'd told her.

But now, Walker just looked beleaguered and deflated. Her heart went out to him. This had to be grueling for him, and Eliza had no way to make it any easier.

''Why don't I drive you home?'' she proposed. ''We can call it a night.''

They'd done that for five days running, and he'd agreed each time to her suggestion because there'd been such a long string of names left to go through. But this time was different. This time they were nearing the end, and he kept hoping that this long shot of hers was going to pay off.

Subtly, he rotated his shoulders, trying to get the stiffness out. ''How many names are left on the list?''

''Two. We can do them in the morning,'' Eliza said again.

Walker wasn't about to be put off. ''We can do them now.''

The commanding note in his voice was positively chilling. She could see his underlings jumping to attention whenever he spoke to them in that tone. She laughed softly. "If I were a soldier, I would have saluted you just now."

"Sorry." He hadn't meant to bark at her like that. "It's just that I have a feeling we're so close..." Walker said.

He didn't need to explain. The man had a right to his frustration. She'd probably have felt the same in his place. "No problem."

It was hard to feel justified over losing control of his temper when she continued to absolve him like that. Walker looked at her, a smattering of curiosity surfacing. He figured it was a way to cut into the silence. "Were there any soldiers in your family?"

"My dad." She wasn't sure if her father really qualified for the title. It wasn't as if he'd started out being a career soldier. "But only for one tour of duty. My grandfather talked him into enlisting, thinking that the army would make him settle down." Her grandfather had made no secret of his annoyance at the son who had dropped out of school, moving aimlessly from job to job. "He met my mother while he was stationed in Georgia." Eliza smiled, remembering her mother's tales. They'd come in the form of bedtime stories: the handsome soldier and the kindergarten teacher. Eliza had loved them. "I think she fell for the uniform and he fell for her southern accent."

Didn't sound as if they'd had much in common; still, Walker felt compelled to say something positive. "Marriages have been built on less."

"And more," she countered. Her parents would

have been happier had there been more common ground for them. "Although God knows she tried to make a go of it. She just never knew what he wanted." Eliza pushed back the sadness that insisted on finding her. Her parents were both gone; there was no reason to dwell on the negative. "Neither did he, I think. That's what made it so hard."

Walker felt a stirring of sympathy and had no idea what to do with it, or how to express it. He wasn't good at things like that. "Are you an only child?"

"I think my father called me 'an only mistake.'" Eliza saw a streak of anger cross Walker's brow and wondered if he was aware of it. "But to answer your question, I have no brothers or sisters. How about you?"

"A sister. Older. Just by two years, but Patrice always thinks she knows what's best." He wondered what Eliza would say if she knew that Patrice had argued heatedly against his getting back on this numbing merry-go-round ride.

"Bosses you around?" Even as she asked, Eliza couldn't picture anyone attempting to tell Walker what to do.

"She used to." When they were growing up, he would have sworn Patrice was the bossiest person on the face of the earth. Certainly the bossiest sister. "Now she calls it 'constructive input.'"

Eliza heard the fond note in his voice. "Sounds as if you're close."

Walker shrugged, looking through the window on the passenger side. "She lives in Newport Beach."

That wasn't really an answer. The man was evasive. She wondered if his emotions had always been wrapped up so tightly, or if the kidnapping had done it to him. "I didn't mean proximity."

"I know what you meant, I just…" His voice trailed off. He wasn't accustomed to admitting anything this personal, even his attachment to a sister who meant a great deal to him. He'd never been overly demonstrative, and in the past two years he'd shut himself away almost completely. He was sure he was empty inside.

If that were true, why had he kissed Eliza? a small voice mocked him. He chose not to listen.

"Do you realize that we've been riding around in this car for essentially five-and-a-half days and that's the longest conversation we've had? Certainly the most personal one," Eliza commented.

Yes, he realized it. He hadn't meant to go on like that. Walker shifted in his seat, still staring out the window. "Won't happen again."

"Why?"

He looked at her, unable to make heads or tails out of the single-word enquiry. "I thought you mentioned it because it made you uncomfortable."

If anyone was uncomfortable about it, it was him. The same instinct that had her bringing home wounded animals at a very young age made her want to help Walker.

"I was just noting the conversation for posterity. I don't mind personal conversations, Walker. The professional part of our relationship comes in with my finding Bonnie, but there's no rule against our talking to each other or becoming friends."

"Friends?" He was on a first-name basis with a great many of the people he worked with. He didn't think of any of them as friends, not really. Why should she be any different?

"Friends are easier to talk to than strangers," Eliza said.

He shrugged, wishing the woman would do what he was paying her to do and not venture into areas she had no business being in. Served him right for making conversation, he admonished himself.

"I'm not accustomed to doing much talking outside the parameters of business."

"That's a pity." The note of regret in her voice was sincere. "You have a definite knack for it." When he made no comment, she knew she'd embarrassed him. It hadn't been her intention. "You're sure you wouldn't rather see these last two families when you're fresher?"

"I just want to get this over with."

Over with. It occurred to Eliza that she should say a few words to prepare him in case the last two interviews led them nowhere, just like the others had. But she knew he wouldn't appreciate it. More than likely, he'd think she was talking down to him.

He was intelligent enough, she reasoned, to know

that this was a shot in the dark. One of many they might have to take before Bonnie was finally found.

She hoped he was up to them.

They had no luck with the second-to-last name on their list.

Or with the last one, either.

The tall, thin woman who had met them at the door had deep, dark circles under her eyes and the dull, vacant stare of someone who had not recovered from her loss. She appeared to be living alone in the house, except for a small dog that barked incessantly in the background. Fay Kelley chased them away, screaming after them and calling them ghouls for coming around to ask about her daughter. She slammed the door in their wake.

"Maybe you should have her checked out further," Walker said to her as they walked back to Eliza's car at the curb.

Eliza knew what he was doing. He was trying to hang on to hope. But this wasn't where Walker would find it.

Eliza shook her head. "Bonnie's not here."

"How do you know?" he demanded. Frustrated, he waved his hand toward the house they'd just walked away from. "You never even went inside. What, the rays didn't come permeating out to meet you? You didn't get the right 'vibes'?"

"No," she told him quietly, knowing he had to get this out of his system, "I didn't."

"You know, the hell with your vibes, the hell with everything." Angrily, Walker stormed past her car.

He caught her off guard. It took her a second to recover. "Walker, get in the car," she called out after him.

He didn't bother turning around. "No. I'll walk home."

Eliza raised her voice. "It's fifteen miles from here."

Right now, he felt as if he could use the distraction. "I'll make good time. I was on the high school track and field team."

With a shake of her head, Eliza quickly got into the car and started it up. When she caught up to Walker, she slowed her vehicle down to match his pace. "Be reasonable."

Walking briskly, he didn't look in her direction, even though the car remained parallel to him. "I am being reasonable, I need to work off this steam."

Eliza swerved to miss a parked car at the curb. "You have no steam to work off. It barely qualifies as a wisp rising out of a tepid kettle. And besides, I wasn't referring to that, anyway."

That caught his attention. He slowed his pace and spared a glance in her direction. "What were you talking about, then?"

Leaning over, one hand on the steering wheel, Eliza unlocked the passenger door. "Why don't you get in and I'll tell you?"

He debated holding his ground, but she was right.

He was being stubborn and he was tired. More tired than he'd ever thought possible. His exhaustion went clear down to the bone.

Curbing a sudden, fresh onslaught of anger, he bit off a curse, opened the door and got in.

His eyes were dark as he looked at her. "All right, I'm in. Talk."

She ignored the belligerent tone. "When I asked you to be reasonable, I meant about this being a long shot. We both knew there was a huge chance we were going to come up empty." She looked at him. She didn't need the streetlights or her intuition to know that he was struggling to maintain his temper. No one could blame him. "It's only natural for you to hope otherwise, so did I, but the odds weren't in our favor."

Walker pressed the button on the armrest and rolled down a window. He needed air to clear his head. It didn't really help. "And just when do they get to be in our favor?"

"They don't." That was the problem. The only supposed "sure thing" in this mix was her, and she knew he didn't want to hear that. "We just keep going against them until we find her."

"Anyone ever tell you you talk in riddles?" Or maybe he was just too tired to follow her.

"I'm a clairvoyant, I'm supposed to be mysterious." She looked to see if she'd gotten a glimmer of a smile out of him. She hadn't. "Sorry, I couldn't resist. Just in case you haven't noticed, I'm trying to lighten the mood.''

He knew that she was and that his behavior wouldn't win any gold stars, but he wasn't exactly feeling congenial right now. He'd really begun to hope that maybe she was on to something. He should have known better.

''You're wasting your time, Eliza. I'm not interested in lightening the mood. There's only one thing I'm interested in.''

''Yes, I know. So am I.'' She paused, weighing her words carefully, knowing that no matter what, he wasn't going to like what she was about to say. ''Look, Walker, this can't be any good for you. Why don't we leave it at this? I promise I'll call you as soon as I have a viable lead.''

He didn't work that way, and he wasn't about to let her think that he did. Shifting in his seat, he turned until the seat belt strained against his shoulder.

''Look, until you came to my door last week, I had gotten my life back in some kind of order and on track. I'd resigned myself to accepting certain facts. And then you came in like gangbusters, talking about dreams and visions and whatever the hell else you claimed, and even though I knew logically that it was all just a bunch of bull, I let myself get sucked in. Let myself hope again that Bonnie was alive because you said she was.'' He sank down in his seat again, staring straight ahead. ''I should have had my head examined.''

"It's not your head that's at stake here, Walker, it's your heart." The look he gave her was dark, but she continued, anyway. "It's your heart that believes Bonnie is still alive, your heart that isn't convinced she's gone."

She was bandying words about. "Head, heart— what does it matter?"

"It matters a great deal, Walker," she insisted, "because it's the heart that causes miracles to happen." The cynical look on his face only encouraged her. "It's because the heart refuses to give up that people wake up from comas, that permanently crippled people walk, that—"

He didn't want to hear any more. He was *this* close to telling her where to go.

"Don't you ever stop?" he demanded. "Maybe I don't want all this hope thrown at me. Maybe I just want to make my peace with reality. All your babbling is giving me one hell of a headache so I really wish you'd just back off."

She pressed her lips together, retreating. What he'd just said had reminded her too much of words her father had thrown at her. Words that had been just as hurtful.

"All right," she agreed quietly.

Eliza concentrated on the road. Traffic was beginning to thin out, and if she sped up she'd make good time. They both needed a breather.

This wasn't going to work, she thought. She couldn't try to make progress on one hand and deal with Walker's skepticism on the other. She needed a clear head if she was going to find Bonnie.

Maybe the debate was moot. For all she knew, when she dropped him off, Walker was going to terminate their association. Which would be just as well. She didn't intend to drop the investigation, but she would make far more headway without Walker along. At the very least, he'd been a distraction. There were thoughts, feelings, emotions circling her that had nothing to do with the investigation, and she couldn't afford to be split this way.

She needed to pay attention to signs along the way, not to a darkly brooding man, no matter how good-looking he was.

They rode in silence all the way to Walker's house, but when she stopped the car in his driveway, he didn't get out immediately.

This was awkward. He forced himself to face her. He owed her that much. Hating the way every word made him feel, he began haltingly. "Listen, I had no right to shout at you like that."

There had never been an angry word uttered that she couldn't forgive if asked to. She supposed that was probably why her father had called her to his deathbed. He'd known she'd forgive him.

"You're under a strain," she allowed.

He would have felt better if she'd yelled back at him, or vented now. This drilled holes into his conscience, holes that filled up with guilt.

"That's no excuse, and I really wish you'd stop being so forgiving." He was certain he'd never met anyone quite like her, clairvoyance notwithstanding. "Don't you ever get angry?"

She shook her head. "Waste of time and energy," she replied.

She meant that, he thought. The woman was incredible. "The rest of us haven't tapped into sainthood yet," he confessed. "In case I'm doing a lousy job, you should know I'm trying to apologize."

"I know. And I told you once, you don't have to apologize to me."

"Yes, I do," he contradicted. Walker lifted her chin to inspect her expression. He was no expert on women, and heaven knows, even if he were, he wouldn't be able to understand this one—but he could tell the signs of hurt when he saw them. He'd seen them often enough on Rachel's face and had ignored them. And that would be a guilt he would bear forever. "And I want to give them. I didn't mean to yell at you that way."

Her shrug was small, delicate. "You're not the first."

He tried to read between the lines. Was she referring to a man in her life? Like a pebble suddenly picked up in his shoe, the thought unexpectedly bothered him. "Then tell him he shouldn't."

"He's gone. And I could never tell my father anything, even when he was alive."

The relief, too, was unexpected. "Your father?"

She nodded. "He would have made you look like a piker. So, don't beat yourself up about raising your voice at me. I've been subjected to the worst and emerged unscathed."

Her answer left him wondering about her even after she drove away.

Chapter 9

Walker got out of his car, slamming the door shut behind him. Several people in the parking lot looked in his direction, but he ignored them. There was no containing his irritation.

After Bonnie had been kidnapped and Rachel had committed suicide, it was as if all his emotions had somehow drained out of him. There were no highs, no lows in his life from there on in, just one flat line. Along with that was an endless parade of days that fed into each other, marked by the rising and setting of the sun, and work—nothing more.

But ever since Eliza had knocked on his door, he'd found himself unwillingly holding a Pandora's box. All his emotions had suddenly come flying out like jet-propelled spirits.

And anger had headed the list.

This time, the anger was not aimless. Anger had a direction. *Eliza.*

In lieu of Eliza—because he was certain she'd gone off somewhere—he intended to give whomever he found in the office one hell of a dressing down for being treated the way he had been. In the past week he'd come to expect more from a firm that had such an impressive reputation and track record.

He stormed into the reception area like Hurricane Andrew taking Florida.

"She's not in, is she?" he demanded without a preamble, his words directed at the petite secretary sitting behind the desk.

Startled, recognition entered Carrie's dark eyes. She offered a tentative smile as she made the connection. "It's Mr. Banacek, right?"

His hands splayed on either side of Carrie's desk, he leaned forward, measuring out each word. "I know who I am—" he glanced at her name plate "—Ms. Scott. I wanted to know where Eliza Eldridge is."

"I'm right here."

The cool, soft voice was in sharp contrast to his own. Caught off guard, Walker looked to his left and saw Eliza standing in the doorway of her office. Framed in sunlight thanks to the orientation of her corner office, she looked like one of the blithe spirits that inhabited children's fairy tales. Angry as he was, the stray thought that she should be wearing something diaphanous, dipped in pale, peach colors, came out of nowhere and surprised the hell out of him.

Her appearance took some of the wind out of his sails. Retreating from Carrie's desk, he straightened and turned toward Eliza. "So I see."

She'd spent the night in her office, poring over files and catching catnaps on the small sofa she kept there. Rusty had been prompt with his findings—which had led nowhere. And there had been all those files previously compiled on the case. Megan had managed to obtain them for Eliza via her connections at the FBI. They'd needed to be gone over, just in case someone had missed something the first time around.

Eliza had read until her eyes felt as if they were crossing.

The catnap on the sofa ended when she'd had the dream about Bonnie again. After that, she just kept on working. Cade had a shower in the bathroom in his office and she'd availed herself of that before anyone had come in this morning.

She'd known Walker was coming the moment he'd set foot in the elevator. She'd just felt it. Funny how well she could read him. That had only happened once before, with her mother. Not that it had done her mother any good.

His eyes were dark when he turned them on her. There was another storm brewing, she thought. "What are you doing here?" she asked.

Clearly not in the mood for conversation, Walker strode over to her. "I spent half the morning straining to hear my cell phone ringing, waiting for you to call me. I must have checked it half a dozen times to see if it was working.'' The dark eyes pinned her. ''Why haven't you called me?''

''I didn't have anything to call you about.'' She still didn't, not really. But he was here now, and she knew he wouldn't just leave if she told him to. That wasn't him. She moved back from the doorway. ''Why don't we step into my office?''

She saw Carrie looking at her, one eyebrow raised in a silent query. She knew what the secretary was asking. If she needed Carrie to call someone for help. That wasn't going to be necessary. She could take care of Walker Banacek on her own.

Eliza shook her head, then closed the door.

Walker was by her desk, waiting for her. He flipped through the list of people Savannah had compiled for her last week. ''We've talked to everyone on that list you made up, right?''

She crossed to the other side of her desk, automatically straightening the files into stacks. Somewhere toward three in the morning, neatness had stopped counting. ''Yes.''

''So where do we go from here?'' Without waiting for her answer, he picked up one of the files she'd just stacked and flipped through it. The date jumped out at him. ''Are these the old files?''

She nodded. ''One of our operatives, Megan, used to work for the FBI. She pulled a few strings, got us the files. I thought they might help.'' *Or at least keep us from recrossing old ground,* she added silently.

''The FBI just *gave* you all of them?'' Walker asked. They hadn't been willing to share anything while they were working the case, just counseling him to be patient and to let them do their job.

''Not exactly,'' Eliza replied evasively, ''but we have them.''

Glancing by her desk, he saw that there were boxes filled with files behind her, boxes that hadn't been there the last time he'd been in her office. ''How?''

She sidestepped the answer. ''Some things are better left unsaid.''

Though there was something about Walker Banacek she trusted implicitly, the explanation as to how the material had gotten to her desk wasn't hers to give. It had taken the combined efforts of Megan and Savannah. Especially Savannah. Sam's wife was invaluable to the office, and whatever methods she used to access information for them were her own business. Eliza wasn't about to turn the spotlight on her.

Eliza was a woman who could keep a secret, Walker thought. He rather liked that. ''I can respect that.'' Squatting down, he gave the first box a cursory rummaging. There was a lot here. ''How long will it take you to get through all this?'' He tried not to sound as impatient as he felt, but wasn't sure if he was successful. In any event, he was beginning to believe she could read between the lines better than most.

"I already have."

There looked to be several thousand pages here. Eliza had to be putting him on, Walker thought. "How, by passing your hand over them?"

The man could definitely do with a refresher course in charm. "No, by speed reading. Comes in handy in my line of work."

She didn't add that it had also come in handy when she was studying, or that she'd graduated from college at the age of twenty-four with a PhD in paranormal psychology. Intelligence tended to frighten people away, and she was already laboring under one handicap; she didn't want another one with him.

He took a closer look at her. "Have you gotten any sleep?"

"Some." She looked at him pointedly. "And when I did, I had that dream again."

He didn't want to talk about the dream. At the moment, he didn't think he was up to hearing about his daughter calling to him. Instead, he gestured toward the boxed files.

"Did you find anything there that...?"

Very slowly, Eliza shook her head.

Impatience rose another notch. "So where are we, back to square one?"

"Not exactly." She'd been mulling over this latest idea for the past hour. Right now, it seemed the only way to go. "I told you I had that dream again last night. Each time I have it, it becomes a little clearer. This time, it was so vivid, I could sketch the details if I had to.'' She closed her eyes now, summoning the images as she'd seen them. ''There's tall grass, tall enough to reach a six-year-old's hips, and a dilapidated farmhouse in the distance. Near it is a barn with no door, as if the animals left and are never coming back.''

With her eyes closed like that, reciting, she almost seemed as if she was in a trance. Sleeping Beauty, he thought, only with words.

Walker roused himself. He wasn't supposed to get distracted by the seer, but concentrate on what she had seen. And what she had seen wasn't very helpful. ''You're describing a scene that could be found anywhere in about thirty of the fifty states,'' Walker commented.

''I know, I know, but I have a feeling it's here.''

He surprised her by not waving away the notion. She was getting him to come around, she thought with a sense of triumph.

''Here? As in Southern California?''

What she was feeling told her it was even closer than that. ''As in Tustin, or maybe the older parts of San Juan Capistrano.''

''So what are you going to do about it?'' he asked.

She slipped a map into her purse. ''Find it.''

That was what they both ultimately wanted to do, but she still hadn't answered his question.

''How?''

She came around from behind her desk and joined him. ''By driving around.''

He stared at her incredulously. Just when he was beginning to think she made sense, she said something like this. "What, aimlessly?"

She trusted her instincts. Somehow, she'd know if she was going in the right direction. Something would tell her. She had complete faith in that. She had to. "In part."

He didn't know whether to laugh at her and walk out, or just follow her. "Don't you even get a divining rod?"

Her smile was soft, and he felt something within him being pulled toward her, even though he didn't want it to be. "I guess I am the divining rod."

He wasn't exactly sure how the small bit of distance between them had disappeared, but it had. He was standing much too close to her to think clearly. "Does that mean I'm supposed to hold on to you?"

Eliza raised her head until her eyes just seemed to touch his. There was warmth shimmering in them. "Not while I'm driving."

Her choice of words intrigued him.

They took his car this time, so that she could concentrate solely on looking, on searching. Walker had spent the better part of his life in Southern California, but there were regions he'd never ventured into. So he had no knowledge of the old farmlands that still dotted the land, disappearing slowly like some soon-to-be-extinct breed. He'd been only vaguely aware that once all of the ever-growing Orange County had been fertile farmlands.

Armed with the map, they drove through the winding back roads of Tustin and along the terrain that buffed Lake Elisnore, until the light finally began to give out. They passed farms, some run-down, but all occupied, and fields. Each time they did, he would look at her, waiting. Each time, she shook her head.

As dusk descended, his mounting disappointment became almost palatable.

Eliza bit her lower lip, holding back her own frustration. She'd been so sure she could find it. "I'm sorry."

The apology sounded sincere. He glanced at her and noted how wan she looked. When they'd stopped to get something to eat, she'd hardly touched her food. She was that intent on what she was doing. Finding a child she didn't even know.

Walker set his own feelings aside. "Nothing to feel sorry about. You're doing your best."

It was the first time she'd heard him say something like that. Touched, she reached out and placed her hand on his arm. A commercial about milk came on the radio. A cow was lowing in the background.

The sound grew louder, drowning out the people who were talking, filling her head.

Walker glanced at Eliza, and his words faded from his lips. Her face had gone completely ashen and her eyes were glazed, as if she was seeing something. But there was nothing to see, just open road beginning to be wrapped in darkness.

Concerned, he pulled over. "Are you all right?"

When she didn't answer, he took hold of her shoulders, gently shaking her. "Eliza?"

She heard his voice coming to her from a great distance and forced herself to reach out to it. To him. She blinked several times, until his face finally came into focus. She felt exhausted, as if she'd been running a long way. Exhausted and exhilarated. She knew.

"Bedford," she whispered half to herself, half to him. "They never left Bedford after they took her." Her voice grew stronger. "There's a farm on the other end, near the foothills, in Old Bedford."

He didn't think to doubt her. "Which way?"

"That way." With no hesitation, she pointed north. He drove.

There were no lights coming from the farmhouse as they approached. It stood almost shyly on the land it had once graced, a forgotten relic from an era gone by. The weed grass that surrounded it went on forever and was as high as she had described it. High enough to brush against a six-year-old's hips.

He'd been the one to point out that there were hundreds of places that fit the sketchy description she'd given, but at the sight of it, his heart pounded, anyway.

He wanted to believe. With all his heart, he wanted to believe.

Eliza could sense the change in him, and it energized her. Tangled with her desire to find the missing girl was the very real feeling that she didn't want to disappoint him. She wanted to end his suffering.

Walker looked at her. "Well?" The single word thundered like a demand, though he hadn't meant it to sound that way.

She nodded. "It's the one."

"Are you sure?" Even as he asked, he pressed down on the accelerator, eating up the distance between them and the structure.

Her eyes never left the farmhouse as it came closer to them. "I'm sure."

Walker let the certainty in her voice guide him. Hope battled against logic. There were no lights. If Bonnie was there, did that mean...?

He wouldn't let himself finish the thought.

Pulling up in front of the house, he leaped out of his car, agitation making him abandon decorum. "There's a flashlight in the glove compartment," he told Eliza. "Get it." He hurried up the wooden steps, calling his daughter's name. "Bonnie? Bonnie, are you in there? Bonnie, it's Daddy!"

Right behind him, Eliza grabbed his hand and pulled him back, just as the last step broke apart beneath his foot. If she hadn't stopped him in time, he would have gone right through.

Jolted, trying to regain his self-control, his emotions running rampant, he looked at her. "Thanks."

She had no time to answer him.

Walker was pounding on the door. The second time he banged his fist against the surface, the door flew open. It hadn't been locked.

A sinking feeling took hold of his gut.

"Bonnie? Bonnie, are you in here, baby?" He struggled to keep fear from overpowering him. "Hello, is *anyone* here?"

Taking the flashlight from Eliza, he made his way from room to room. He called to his daughter, or to anyone who might hear.

No one answered.

Walker looked for signs that Bonnie had been here, or that any child had played recently in this rotting house. Room after room within the single-story, sparsely furnished house turned up empty. There was nothing to feed his hope.

He stopped in the last room of the house—a kitchen that looked as if it hadn't been updated since the early forties—and turned around to look at the woman who had shadowed his every step.

"If they were even here, they left a long time ago."

Not that long ago, she thought. There had been people living here within the past year. "They were here."

He wanted to believe her, but she was going to have to help him. He needed reasons. "And how can you be so sure?"

"Look over there—" She pointed to the window over the sink.

The dirt on the panes made it almost impossible to see out, especially in the growing dark. Walker rubbed the dirt away with the flat of his hand and looked out. There was a structure several yards from the house. Squinting, he realized it was a barn. There was no door. Given the state of disrepair, it wasn't unusual.

"Doesn't prove anything," he told her.

It did to her. "There should be an oak tree in the field behind the house."

Skepticism refused to let go. "All right, let's go see."

Walker began to go to the front of the house. He intended to drive around to the back and to the oak tree that might or might not be there. In either case, he figured they could use the headlights from the car for illumination.

But as he began to walk, he heard the creak of the back door as it opened and then closed again. He turned around. "Eliza?"

She was gone.

"Now she's Houdini." Muttering under his breath, Walker hurried after her down back stairs that had lost their railing a long time ago. "Eliza!"

She didn't answer him. Instead, she was running away from him and through the grass.

Walker made out her form in the dimming light and marveled at the distance she had already put between them. He'd had no idea she could move that fast. The woman was a font of talents, he thought, breaking into a run himself.

He caught up to her at the tree, not even realizing, at first, that it was there. His attention was focused on Eliza.

Grabbing her arm, he turned her around. "Didn't you hear me calling you?"

She was breathing hard, her chest heaving. "Yes, but I knew you'd follow."

He tried to ignore the rhythmic movement. How could he be attracted to her at a time like this? What was wrong with him? he upbraided himself.

"Why were you running? The tree wasn't going anywhere." And then he stopped to look as the import of his own words hit him. "The oak tree."

She nodded, catching her breath. "The oak tree."

He stepped back, looking at her with something akin to awe and just a hint of unease. "Is it...where you saw it in your dream?"

She walked backward, away from him and the tree, keeping the farmhouse in the distance. Framing the scene in her mind.

"Yes." Eliza stared at the tree as if it were an entity that could communicate. Crossing back to it, she ran her hand along the rough bark. A warmth sprang to her fingertips. "Bonnie leaned against this tree, trying to hide from someone. This was where she was when she was calling to you."

Each word stabbed at his heart. His little girl had

been here, sometime after the kidnapping. Crying for him. And he hadn't been able to come to her.

Walker curled his hands at his sides, trying to control emotions that threatened to erupt. The urge to kill was very strong, but there was no outlet. He banked it down.

He became aware that Eliza had dropped to her hands and knees and was searching for something in the dark around the base of the tree.

He crouched to her level. "What are you looking for?"

Eliza rocked back on her heels. She wasn't looking. She had found it.

"This—"

She held up her trophy. Moving in the breeze was a dirty piece of pink ribbon—the kind that might once have been attached to a little girl's toe shoe.

Chapter 10

Like a man in a trance, Walker reached for the ribbon Eliza had in her fingers.

Taking it from her, he held the slender scrap of material in the palm of his hand as if it were a fragile flower. His heart pounding, he stared at it for several moments as twilight ushered dusk away.

The only light came from the moon. The flashlight he'd used to illuminate their way through the farmhouse and the field had fallen from his lax fingers when Eliza had held up the ribbon.

Bonnie's ribbon.

Logic would have placed the odds against the ribbon actually being a broken lace from Bonnie's toe shoe. There were no real identifying marks. A pink ribbon was a pink ribbon, nothing more. It could have come from a dress, from a wayward pigtail...

And yet he knew it had belonged to his daughter. Knew with a certainty burning in his gut.

He looked up at Eliza. The brightness of her eyes was not diminished by the lack of light. They seemed to shine right into his, saying things to him that came from her heart even though her lips never moved.

She knew, he thought. Even before him.

Still, he heard himself saying, "It's Bonnie's," half in question, half in firm statement.

"It's Bonnie's," she replied, the quiet tone of her voice belying the excitement she felt. Though Eliza had been sure they were on the right trail coming to this farm, it was gratifying to find evidence that proved her right. Just touching the ribbon had brought visions of Bonnie to her.

He closed his hand over the ribbon. So near and yet so damn far. Where *was* she?

"But Bonnie's not here. How do we—?" The very question choked him, and he was unable to think, he who had always been able to arrive at logical conclusions so easily.

But logic had nothing to do with this—neither with his daughter's abrupt disappearance, nor the appearance of this fey woman in his life.

"We go to the county records office in the morning and find out who owns this piece of property. We'll track him or her down," she promised. She didn't know if the owner had been the one who kidnapped Bonnie, but he or she knew something about the abduction—that much she could swear to.

Maybe it was the moonlight, but she thought she saw tears shimmering in Walker's eyes. For a moment, Eliza didn't know how to proceed, whether to acknowledge the tears, or ignore them and give Walker his privacy. Even from her limited experience, she knew men weren't big on showing emotion. In all likelihood, Walker probably would prefer if she just pretended she didn't notice.

But the immense capacity she had for empathy overwhelmed any practical judgment she was wrestling with. Eliza covered the tight fist that was holding Bonnie's pink ribbon with her own and gave it a gentle squeeze.

Struggling with his thoughts, Walker raised his eyes to hers again. He could feel her empathy, feel her excitement. It was as if she were telegraphing it to him somehow.

His breath caught in his throat.

Was it the emotion-packed moment that had him hallucinating this way, or was there something about this woman that spoke to him? Something that delved into his innermost being and somehow connected with what he kept hidden there?

Walker's head began to hurt.

He couldn't deal with all that, with the import of what these jumbled thoughts he was having might mean. He was accustomed to dealing with facts and the reality he could see.

Still, there was something…

He made no movement to withdraw his hand, enjoying, instead, the warmth he felt emanating from her. "Thank you."

His thanks embarrassed her. She hadn't yet accomplished what she'd set out to do. "Save that for when we find her."

When, always "when," not "if." Eliza was such a positive force that she seemed to sap the energy out of the negative thoughts that resided in his mind, the negative aura he had lived with for so long. He'd never been accused of being a happy-go-lucky person, but the double tragedy that had upended his life had sent him plummeting down to the fiery depths of a hell few could actually imagine. With her continuously optimistic outlook, Eliza was like his lifeline back to the land of the living.

He continued to be mesmerized by her eyes. "You're always so positive. Doesn't being up all the time tire you out?"

It would if it were a conscious effort. But it wasn't. It was just the way she approached things. "On the contrary, it helps make the bad things in life bearable, and it energizes me."

"Energize," he repeated, laughing shortly, acutely aware of the fact that her hand was still on his. "You've got enough energy for both of us."

"That's the idea."

Suddenly realizing that her hand was still covering his, Eliza dropped hers to her side.

Almost shyly, he thought, watching her turn away to lead the way back to the farmhouse and his car.

There were so many things going on inside him right now, he couldn't begin to put a label on them.

And Eliza was responsible. For all of it.

"Eliza," he whispered.

She turned around, not looking quite as confident as she had a moment ago. Looking, it occurred to him, almost vulnerable. Why, he had no idea. But he knew that what he saw caused an overwhelming surge of feeling within him.

The next moment, still holding the ribbon, Walker framed her face with his hands and then lightly kissed her lips.

That was all it was supposed to be. A small kiss born of gratitude, of happiness for being able to hope again, for even just a little while.

But contact had added something else to the mix. Kissing her once made him want to kiss her again. And again.

Slipping the ribbon in his pocket, he took her into his arms and deepened the kiss, turning a single lyric into a song and then a symphony.

Kissing her satisfied nothing, ended nothing. Instead, it unleashed a ravenous hunger he hadn't been aware of harboring.

It made him want to make love with her.

The realization scorched him, as if someone had suddenly raked a red-hot poker over his flesh. Jolted, he backed away, his eyes wide as he looked at her.

He could only guess what she must think of him. "I didn't mean to get carried away."

It took Eliza a second to catch her breath. Walker's kiss had depleted her lungs even as it had filled her body with the most delicious sensations.

"I didn't mind," she murmured.

Was that wrong? Should she have said something witty that would put this all back on a strictly business level?

But it wasn't on a strictly business level. She couldn't divorce herself like that, couldn't place Walker and the case into a neat little box and seal a lid over it. Not when she was spending her emotions like this. Not when she was turning herself inside out and using every shred of her being to uncover his daughter's whereabouts.

An awkwardness slipped over Walker. He shouldn't have done that, no matter what she said. "I guess I'd better drive you home."

It was the moment that had caused him to get carried away, he thought, promising himself to be in control again by the morning.

"You'd better," she agreed with a smile. "It's a long walk from here."

He looked at her oddly, then dismissed her words with a shake of his head. He didn't know why Eliza's having a sense of humor took him unawares the way it did. He just didn't expect it from someone like her.

The path back to the house was uneven, made worse by the darkness. Eliza was surprised when he took her arm. Surprised and pleased.

* * *

The sound of the doorbell made its way into the kitchen. Eliza glanced at the wall clock: 7:05. Later than expected, she mused, making her way to the front of the house.

Granted, seven in the morning was not a time when she ordinarily entertained company, but after last night's find, she'd assumed Walker would be champing at the bit to get going.

She wasn't disappointed.

He was on her doorstep, a man in conflict, nonetheless eager to set wheels into motion. The conflict, she sensed, had to do with her.

She'd already made up her mind to make it as easy as she could for him, pretending that he hadn't kissed her almost senseless last night. Pretending that the last dream she'd had before waking up hadn't been of him. Of things, she thought, that probably would never be.

She had no way of knowing, one way or the other. It would be nice, she mused, if the abilities that allowed her to glimpse both the past and the future of other people's lives would allow her to see into her own life once in a while. But it was as if that somehow was forbidden by the rules of this game she was compelled to play. She could peer into other people's lives, but her own remained a mystery.

She opened the door. "I expected you about half an hour ago."

The woman had the ability to render him speechless. "Really?"

She could almost see his mind working, chewing on her words. "Logical deduction," she told him before he could ask. "Come on in." Eliza stepped back, allowing him access, then closed the door behind him. For once, his common sense appeared to have deserted him. She rather liked that. "You do realize that government offices do not open up at seven, probably not even for the president."

Yes, he realized that he was early. Realized, too, though he wasn't quite sure how, that she'd be up at this hour. Maybe it had been wishful thinking.

"I couldn't sleep," he confessed.

Most of it had been due to the excitement over finding the ribbon, which was now in his right pants pocket, tucked away there for luck. But some of it had been because of Eliza, because of what he had felt when he had kissed her. He tried to tell himself that what he was feeling was because of the situation. It was the victim–rescuer, patient–doctor mentality that caused a person to see someone who came to their aid in less than realistic terms, turning them into a god-like being. Or, in Eliza's case, a goddess-like being.

But somehow, all the logical arguments he had used on himself had not managed to penetrate his mind. They certainly hadn't been able to erase the feeling that was within him now.

He wanted to be with her. Intimately.

The last part crept up on him unannounced, and he banked it down. What the hell was wrong with him?

They were looking for his daughter. How could he be thinking of making love to a woman in the middle of all this? Was he losing all reason?

He was going to have to exercise more control over his thoughts, he admonished silently.

Still, looking at her delicate, upturned face, at the compassion in her eyes, it was hard not to be drawn to her.

It occurred to him that this was probably something she encountered on a regular basis. The last thing in the world he wanted was to be some kind of "psychic groupie," especially when the jury was still out over how he felt about such phenomena.

"I was just about to have some coffee," she told him, tightening the robe's sash, which insisted on inopportunely sliding loose. "Would you like some?"

He blew out a breath. "Seeing as how we have no place to go yet, all right."

Walker followed her to the kitchen, trying not to notice how her hips gently swayed beneath the fabric of her silk robe as she led the way. Each step made him warmer. He forced himself to look at the back of her head, instead. A whole lot safer that way, he thought.

"We don't have anyplace to go yet, right?" he prodded, hoping she'd contradict him. Maybe coming here was a bad idea. Meeting her in her office was probably a lot more sensible.

There was a coffeemaker residing on the far end of the pink-and-gray tiled counter. Picking up the coffeepot, Eliza turned to the two cups and saucers she'd taken from the cupboard just before he'd rung the doorbell.

Watching her pour, he realized that she really had been expecting him. Was he as predictable as she had implied, or was that her "gift" telling her he was going to be here?

The question, even without an answer, didn't bother him nearly as much now as it might have a little more than a week ago. Did that mean his thinking was getting more progressive, or that the desperation of the situation had made him suspend logical thinking? He still wasn't certain.

She glanced at him over her shoulder as she poured. "And by 'anyplace,' you mean…?"

"I don't know." He sighed again, shaking his head. "Go back to the farmhouse in the daylight to poke around some more." He looked at her. "Or maybe you had another dream?"

She set the pot back on its burner, buying herself some time before answering. Remembering the dream she'd had. The one with him in it. It had been very vivid, but she knew that it had been created by her own needs, not by her "gift."

Still, thinking about the dream made it difficult to keep the blush from creeping up her neck and coloring her cheeks. Eliza shook her head. "No, no new dream."

The oddest thought that she was holding something back crossed Walker's mind, but he let it go, telling himself he was getting paranoid. So far, Eliza had been incredibly forthcoming, even in the face of his ridicule. She definitely would have told him if there was something to tell, especially since he was encouraging her now.

"How about going back to the farmhouse?" he suggested. Maybe they would find something in the light of day they'd missed in the dark. A flashlight wasn't the best source of illumination.

"We could do that," she agreed slowly. She knew why he wanted to return, but it would just be a waste of energy. She already knew he wasn't destined to find anything more there. "But I think we should save our energy for the county records office. Not everything has been input into the computer yet, and we might have to do some heavy-duty digging."

Moving forward to offer him the coffee she'd poured for him, Eliza caught the edge of her sash on the corner of the counter. At the next step, the silk sash came undone, allowing the two sides of her robe to hang open, framing her body.

He didn't mean to look.

He couldn't help it.

She was wearing a short, lacy nightgown that brushed against the tops of her thighs. The pale pink color contrasted with the light olive cast of her skin.

It also caused Walker to feel as if he were in danger of swallowing his tongue.

He took the cup she was offering him, telling himself again that he was supposed to avert his eyes.

Somehow, he couldn't quite manage the simple action.

"Maybe I should let you get ready," he said, finally able to tear his eyes away from what was, quite likely, the most enticing female form he'd seen in a very long time, and addressing the words to the black liquid in his cup.

"Good idea," she agreed, grateful for the excuse as she started to retreat to her bedroom.

He suddenly became aware of the cup he'd wrapped his hands around. *Coffee. Black.*

"Did you know I took my coffee black, or—?"

The natural assumption would have been that she hadn't had time to offer him any cream or sugar. But, being as how this was Eliza, he knew there was nothing he could assume, naturally or otherwise. As far as he could remember, he hadn't had any coffee while around her, but he could have been wrong there, as well.

In response, Eliza looked over her shoulder at him with what had to be the most enigmatic smile he had ever seen.

Enigmatic or not, he interpreted it. She hadn't needed to see him have coffee to know how he liked it. Some things, obviously, just came to her. Walker still hadn't made up his mind whether he liked that or not, or whether it should even matter how he felt about it.

"Right, dumb question," he muttered under his breath, as she hurried off to get ready.

Chapter 11

The woman behind the counter at the county records office did not look particularly pleased about having to make the effort to communicate with anyone. Sitting at her desk several feet from the counter, she had been oblivious to the sound of the door being opened and then closed when Walker and Eliza came in.

It had taken several attempts to even draw her attention away from the computer monitor she was staring at so intently.

The morning's search did not progress well from there. It had taken twenty minutes for the clerk to grudgingly look for the proper forms Eliza had needed to fill out, before the woman even attempted to search for the deed they were interested in.

Pushing perpetually sliding glasses back up a nose

that was just the slightest bit too short, the woman shook her head. "It's not on here," she informed them from behind the monitor.

"What do you mean, it's not on there?" Walker demanded. He felt Eliza's hand on his arm, silently gentling him. He wasn't interested in being gentled, but he lowered his voice for her sake. "Somebody has to own it."

"Yeah, well, the title hasn't been properly recorded—at least, not in the database," the clerk said.

Now they were entering an area that he had some kind of expertise in. He pointed to the computer. "Are all the deeds for all the county's properties in the database?"

"Not the oldest ones. We started inputting the newest title transfers and worked our way backward."

Transfers. That meant the farmhouse had probably been sold. How recently, and how much more difficult would that make finding Bonnie? he wondered, struggling with a fresh wave of impatience. "And just how far back did you go?"

The clerk hit several keys before replying. "To the beginning of the 1940s."

Eliza was trying to follow the tiny bits of information that were being doled out. "So if this property was owned by one person, or, say, one family, and bought before 1940, it might not have gotten into the database?"

A loud, dramatic sigh escaped before the clerk answered her. "Not yet."

"And just exactly where would the information be?" Walker asked, before Eliza had a chance to.

The clerk's thin lips curled condescendingly. "The archives." She said the word as if it were the last place she would be willing to go.

"And how do we get it from there?" Walker asked, having trouble keeping his voice level.

The woman raised her chin defensively. "You fill out the proper form and—"

More forms. Walker narrowed his eyes. "Bring it on," he instructed.

The woman hesitated, spreading her fingers out along her desk. Like someone stalling for time. Eliza realized the clerk wasn't being difficult, she was being fearful. The easiest assumption was that it had something to do with going down into the archives.

"If we filled the form out, would we be able to go down into the archives ourselves and retrieve the information?" Eliza proposed.

It was obviously the lesser of two evils, if the woman's expression was any indication of the way she felt. But the clerk still hesitated.

"It's highly irregular," she told them with considerably less frost than she had displayed a moment earlier.

"And just what would it take to make it… regular?" At this point, Walker was willing to beg, bribe or browbeat his way to the information.

Beside him, Eliza sneezed. Habit had him reaching for the handkerchief in his pocket. He saw the clerk's eyes light up as she followed the movement. He was more than familiar with the look. Instead of the handkerchief, Walker took out his wallet. The clerk actually managed a smile.

He'd figured she would.

Taking a fifty out of his wallet, Walker folded it over with his thumb and forefinger before sliding his hand over the counter, closer to the records clerk.

No words were exchanged, only the folded bill.

"If you'll just follow me." The woman circumvented the counter and led the way to the door at the rear of the large room. "We keep the archives in the basement," she informed them as she opened the door and ventured down the stairs.

Left with only vague instructions as to which of the many warehouse-like aisles might contain the box with the original deed they were looking for, Eliza and Walker got down to work.

To simplify matters and prevent overlap, they had split up, each taking an aisle. Walker had the one right after Eliza's. After a fruitless hour, he wandered back to where she was working.

Leaning against the dust-laden metal shelves, he watched her. Eliza was diligent and thorough. Both good attributes. So was kindness, he caught himself thinking. "Your intuition doesn't tell you which of these boxes might be the right one, does it?"

She looked up, then rose to her feet. Another box completed. "I only wish it would."

"How long do you think it'll take us to find it?" Walker asked.

She knew he really wanted an answer, but she didn't have one. "That's hard to say. These purchases aren't cross-referenced," she pointed out, sliding the lid back on the box she'd just gone through.

Edging her out of the way, he picked it up and returned it to the space she'd taken it from.

"They boxed them by year, not by lot number, which makes it a lot more difficult," she said.

He dusted off his hands, then decided it was a futile gesture. "Tell me something I don't know," he muttered as he disappeared down the next aisle.

It took them the better part of the morning to track down the name of the owner of the deserted farmhouse. Eliza found it just as she was about to suggest they break for lunch.

"Joseph Garvey," she read aloud, then cried, "Hallelujah!" just before she sank down to the floor, exhaustion weighing her down and interfering with the sense of elation that had overtaken her.

Head buried in a box, Walker thought he heard Eliza's voice. Or maybe he was just hearing things, he decided. But the "hallelujah" definitely caught his attention. "What's that?" he called out.

"Joseph Garvey," she repeated. "He owns the old farmhouse. Or did," she corrected. She'd gotten it from the box marked in a large, bold man's hand: Transferred Titles.

She heard something hit the floor in the next aisle with a *thud*. "Are you all right?" The next moment, she saw Walker peering around the corner.

"Yeah. You found it?" he asked in disbelief.

Eliza held up the faded document. "Right here."

Walker crossed to her quickly. Rather than snatch the document from her, he took it as if he were taking hold of the Holy Grail.

He turned over the deed. "What's this?" There was an 8-by-11 legal document in pristine condition attached to it.

Eliza turned the paper around to look at it. "Looks like the City of Bedford has bought out one Joseph Garvey." She looked at the date of sale. "A little more than four months ago."

The question remained why it hadn't been entered into the computer database, but with so many things falling through the cracks, Eliza was just grateful they had found the deed.

Four months. An eternity when calculated in miles, he thought, taking the paper from her. His daughter could be anywhere. He tried not to let despair get hold of him again, but it wasn't easy.

Walker looked at Eliza, placing his faith in her optimism. "So where do we go from here?"

"We find a way to track down Joseph Garvey." She left the box standing open on the floor. It would be easier to put the document back that way—once she paid to have a copy made. "I doubt very much if we'll get our answer from anyone involved in buying the actual property. In my experience, bureaucrats tend to snow you when you ask the simplest of questions. I never quite figured out why that is,'' she commented, as they made their way up the stairs.

''Long-winded people have to find some kind of work, I guess.''

She looked over her shoulder at him just before opening the stairwell door. He'd made a joke of sorts and didn't even realize it. There was hope for him yet.

That was what it was all about, she thought. Hope.

As it turned out, there was a forwarding address for Garvey, but he was no longer there.

It figured, Walker thought darkly. Nothing about this was going smoothly, but at least for every dead end, there turned out to be a path leading away from it and down another road.

They'd returned to Eliza's office, and she had asked for Savannah's help in locating Garvey's whereabouts. The first thing they uncovered was that there was no driver's license renewal in the DMV records.

Looking over Savannah's shoulder, Eliza mulled over this development. ''If Garvey owned the farm in the thirties, that puts him somewhere in his late eighties, at the least. At that age, he shouldn't be driving around unless he's one sharp old man.'' Something occurred to her. ''This might be a good thing.''

Walker looked at her quizzically.

She hurried to explain. "Unless Garvey's a veteran, in which case he has CHAMPUS coverage, he's on Medicare. We might be able to track him down that way." She placed a hand on Savannah's shoulder. "Savannah, see what you can do with their records."

"Already on it." Switching to another program, Savannah went back online again.

Fifteen minutes later, she had a match.

"Joseph Garvey was a patient at Harris Memorial Hospital two months ago," she announced triumphantly. "He went in with a hip fracture. Had a whole replacement done." She twisted around in her chair to look at the pair who hadn't left her office since she'd begun the online search. "My guess is that the hospital billing department has a current forwarding address for him that might even be more up-to-date than Medicare's."

Walker put his mug of coffee down on Savannah's desk. "Which is?"

"Give me a minute," Savannah said, her fingers flying over the keyboard.

It took her a minute-and-a-half.

Pleased with herself, Savannah leaned back and waved a hand at the computer screen. "Voilà. Joseph Garvey, of the perforated eardrum that kept him out of the service, is presently residing in Bedford Valley Convalescent Home—convalescing."

Eliza and Walker were out the door in less than five minutes.

* * *

They heard Joseph Garvey before they saw him.

A nurse's aide directed them toward the physical therapy room. Approaching it, they heard a deep, rumbling voice complaining that he was being brutalized and abused because he was old and defenseless.

Entering the large room, Eliza and Walker discovered that his voice was the biggest thing about Joseph Garvey. He was on the floor, barely a twig of a man, mounted on an air mattress that bore the markings of thousands of exercises. An agile, muscled man with an incredibly jovial smile was slowly working one of Garvey's legs, softly issuing orders that were not being followed and encouragement that was falling on deaf ears.

"Come on, Mr. Garvey, you'll not be getting any better if you don't try," the physical therapist coaxed.

Garvey frowned. "Don't wanna get better. Fer pity sake, Trevor, I'm ninety-three… Who the hell am I going to get better for?"

Trevor chuckled, all the while working Garvey's leg. "I seen the way Mrs. Masterson was lookin' at you, man. Bet she'd like you to be spry."

"Humph." Despite the sound, the frown softened just a little. "Emma Masterson likes me just the way I am, so I can't get away from her when she comes."

"Then do it so you can get away from her." The therapist shook his head, bringing Garvey's leg up so that the knee bent a little. "Nothin' sadder than a man not bein' a man."

"Stop, stop, you're killin' me." In the middle of the lament, Garvey's attention shifted to the two people who had entered and were standing behind Trevor. "What're you two gawking at?"

Eliza took the initiative. The old man had to be treated with kid gloves, and she had a feeling that with all the stress he'd endured, Walker had left his behind. "Mr. Garvey?"

The scowl returned, but not before the small, sharp eyes had taken in every inch of Eliza. "Unless you're here to tell me that I won the lottery, I'm not talking to anyone."

Trevor shifted around so he could look at them while he continued with Garvey's exercises. "He's Mr. Garvey. Can I help you?"

Putting her hand out, Eliza introduced herself and Walker, then quickly explained the reason for their unannounced visit. Pretending indifference, Garvey nonetheless listened intently.

"We have reason to believe that Mr. Banacek's daughter might have been held on your property several months ago."

Garvey shook his head. "Can't see how that's possible. I lived there until the city decided to make me an offer they thought I couldn't refuse." The puckered face looked by turns genuinely saddened and then angry at the injustice of it. "I would've, if I'da had any help. But that damn grandnephew of mine was always busy at the garage where he claimed he worked. And as for that wife of his, she didn't know how to pick up a dishrag, let alone anything that had to do with farming. I was too old to do it all myself," he complained bitterly. Raising himself up on his elbows, he puffed up his chest. "Ten years ago, I coulda, but that was then, this is now." His eyes shifted to Walker. "Take my advice, don't get old."

Eliza spared a moment to give the old man her sympathy. Something he'd said had caught her attention. "Did your grandnephew always live with you?" It was clear that he thought very little of the man.

"Naw, him and his family came about two, mebbe three years ago, can't say for sure. Alls I know is that they came for the holidays. Least that was what they said. But they stayed on after. Three weeks into the damn visit I find out they've got no place to live. Couldn't just throw them out, even if I wanted to. Which I did," he added honestly.

Squatting down to be on his level, Eliza squeezed Garvey's hand. "You're a good man, Mr. Garvey."

"Damn straight I am. And where did it get me?" He shifted accusing eyes back to his therapist. "Lying on some lumpy mattress, having a sassy kid bark orders at me and pull on my leg like I was some damn rag doll he wanted to play with, or mebbe a piece of taffy."

It was obvious that there was a love–hate relationship going on, one that both men enjoyed, Eliza thought.

But it was something Walker viewed with increasing impatience. Every moment spent here was another moment his daughter was enduring at the hands of her captors. And away from him. He leaned over and said to Eliza, "Where's this getting us?"

She held up her hand, valiantly trying to ignore the shiver his warm breath against her ear had caused. "Mr. Garvey, you mentioned that your grand-nephew—"

"Wallace," he interjected.

She made a mental note of the name, hoping to coax the last one out of Garvey in time. "You mentioned that Wallace had a family. How big a family?"

"Not much, unless you're going by the pound," he cracked, then laughed at his own wit. "His wife was twice his size," he explained once he'd stopped laughing, "but she listened good when he raised his voice."

So far, this was fitting in with the profile Eliza had put together in her mind. "Were there children?"

"Just the one. Girl," Garvey tacked on as an afterthought.

Eliza didn't look at Walker, but she could feel his undercurrent of excitement mounting. "Could you describe her?"

Garvey was beginning to look bored with the line of questioning. "Ain't much good at that."

This time, Eliza looked at Walker. He understood what she wanted from him. He took his wallet out of his pocket, flipping to Bonnie's photograph.

"Did she look anything like this?" he asked the old man.

Taking it from him, Garvey squinted at the photograph. "Yeah, around when they first come." He looked up at Walker. "What're you doing with a picture of Wallace's kid?"

"You said she looked like that when she came," Eliza pressed on gently, as Walker slipped the wallet back into his pocket. "Then she was with your grand-nephew when he and his wife came to spend the holidays with you?"

"Sure, she was with them. Where else would she have been? She was their kid, and a tiny thing at that. Always whimpering and whining. What's this all about, anyway?" he demanded, growing agitated. "Why does he have Miranda's picture?" he glared at Walker.

She thought of making up something because of the man's age and the delicate situation, then decided that maybe the truth would accomplish more. "Your grandnephew and his wife kidnapped Mr. Banacek's daughter."

"You're kiddin'." The words escaped from Trevor.

Garvey looked at them as if they'd lost their minds. "That ain't possible. Wallace and his wife had that kid all along. Hell, my late wife's niece sent us a card one year, telling us her son had had a baby girl, name of Miranda." He nodded his head for emphasis. "'Member her makin' the comment that she hoped having a baby to look after would make Wallace keep his temper better. He was always going off about something or other.''

That could be why there had been that sense of urgency that kept recurring, Eliza thought. Bonnie was afraid of Wallace, with apparent good reason.

''Do you know where Wallace and his family are now?'' she asked, trying not to betray her growing excitement.

Realizing he had the attention of everyone—even Trevor who had temporarily stopped exercising him—Garvey drew out the moment and savored it before shaking his head.

''The three of them lit out a while back when it looked like I was going to lose the farm because I couldn't make no more payments on it. Wallace said something about losing his job at some run-down garage he was working at, but I figured it was because he was afraid I'd ask him for money.'' The disgust in his small, dark eyes was not easy to miss. ''He gimme an address where he'd be staying until he got settled, but I never tried it so I dunno if it's any good or not.''

She wasn't conscious of reaching for Walker's hand, but Walker was. It was as if they had formed some sort of silent bond. Looking for Bonnie had somehow sealed them forever.

''Would you give it to us?'' Eliza asked Garvey.

''Depends.'' Garvey looked at her craftily. ''Whatcha got to trade?''

Walker started to reach for his wallet, but the prospect of money didn't appear to interest the old man. He waved dismissively. The crafty look intensified as he glanced at the physical therapist, then looked up at Eliza.

"You haven't got any chocolate on you, do you?" Garvey asked her eagerly. "They won't let me have chocolate here."

"Mr. Garvey," Trevor began, a kind warning in his voice.

Kind or not, Garvey wasn't about to listen. "See what I mean?"

Eliza remembered having thrown a chocolate bar into her purse for energy. It wasn't like her, and she'd wondered about it at the time, but something had made her do it and she'd learned not to question her own spur-of-the-moment actions too closely. There was usually some sort of reason behind them that would come to light by and by. Like now.

Eliza produced the chocolate bar from her purse. "Will this do?"

His expression showed his disappointment. He'd wanted more. "It'll have to, won't it? Give it here." He reached for it with a scrawny hand.

Eliza held the chocolate bar just out of reach. She was trusting, but she wasn't a fool. "First the address, Mr. Garvey."

He sighed dramatically, then looked at Walker. "You got yourself a sharp one here, boy. Not a bad looker, neither. If I was fifteen years younger and had two good hips, I'd give you a run for your money. Got yourself a paper?'' he asked Eliza.

She already had her pad out. ''Right here.''

''Okay, let's make this fast, before one of those old biddies comes in and wants to share the chocolate with me. Last address I had for that no-account and his family, they were stayin' in Laughlin.'' Garvey rattled off the name of a third-class motel; then, like a child confronted with forbidden fruit, he snatched the chocolate bar from her and eagerly peeled the wrapper back before sinking his teeth, what was left of them, into the candy bar.

The expression on his face was pure ecstasy.

The look on Walker's face, Eliza noted, was hopeful.

Chapter 12

Walker strode quickly through the single aisle of cars in the parking lot behind the convalescent home, eager to get going. Eager to find his daughter and hold her in his arms. The thought that she might not recognize him, might not know him, slipped vaguely through his mind, but he dismissed it. Two years was a long time for a child, but in his heart, he knew she would know who he was.

And if not, he would teach her. He had the rest of his life to teach her. All they had to do was find her. *All.*

The word mocked him as he approached his car and unlocked the driver's side, flipping the lock to allow Eliza to get in on her side. He glanced in Eliza's direction as he got behind the wheel. He doubted that he had ever relied on anyone in his adult life as heavily as he was relying on her now, this small woman with the huge gift.

Eliza slipped her seat belt into place. "Drop me off at my house," she told him, as they left the parking lot. "I need to throw a few things into an overnight bag. I suggest you do the same. I'll meet you at my office in about an hour. We should be able to get a commuter flight to Laughlin."

"That won't be necessary, I have a private plane." It was one of the perks of his position. When the company's stock had split, doubling everyone's portfolio, the board had bought a Learjet to be kept at his disposal. It had barely made an impression. Things no longer mattered to him the way they once had. When there had been someone to share them with.

Eliza laughed softly as they turned onto a main thoroughfare. "Why doesn't that surprise me?"

He made his way around a slow-moving Mercedes. "Probably because you already knew."

The comment unearthed a host of memories. Memories she really didn't want to be reminded of. "No," she said quietly, "I didn't."

There was something in her voice that made him look. Her profile was almost rigid. Walker damned himself for the thoughtless remark. He hadn't meant anything by it.

"Sorry," he mumbled, "didn't mean to strike a nerve. I just assumed that in one way or another, you knew everything." It sounded lame, but it was true.

He just thought, somehow, she could intuit everything and that it was just a sort of strange modesty that kept her from admitting it.

Eliza let out a long breath. She was being too sensitive. "That's all right, you're not the only one who thinks that way."

Funny, though she was a strikingly beautiful woman, he just hadn't thought of her as being involved with anyone. Maybe it was because of all those long hours they had spent together. It just made him think she was single and that she always had been.

"Someone else?"

"Yes."

She wondered how Morgan would have reacted to being thought of as "someone else." Morgan had always considered himself the center of everything, not a peripheral character standing on the sidelines. Maybe that was why he'd left. He couldn't deal with the fact that he wasn't the center of her world the way he wanted to be.

Walker had no idea what was prodding at him, making him curious. If it didn't have to do with micro-data, curiosity didn't normally enter into his world. Yet he heard himself asking, "Someone important?"

"At the time," she admitted. She heard Walker's silent urging to continue. Again she was struck by how in-tune she'd gotten to this quiet man. Despite her gift, it didn't usually happen like this for her.

"Except that when he realized that I wasn't putting him on, that I really did have dreams that turned out to be true, that I could at times see what was going to happen, he couldn't handle it."

It was sadness, not bitterness that welled up within her. Sadness because no matter how hard she'd tried, she'd always been the one on the outside, looking in. Even when she was needed, she was like a consultant, welcomed for the moment, then forgotten.

And it was going to be that way with Walker, she thought.

The sadness threatened to overwhelm her.

"Called me a freak and backed out of my life totally," she finally added. Eliza tried to make light of it. "You'd think with all the things I've been able to intuit, I would at least have seen that coming." Her smile was rueful. "But I didn't."

Without thinking, Walker slipped a hand over hers in silent comfort. "Maybe he wasn't really worth it."

"Maybe," she agreed. "But he seemed worth it at the time."

His hand was back on the wheel. "Anyone serious since then?" Walker realized he was making an effort to sound only vaguely interested instead of as interested as he actually was.

"Nope. I got too busy." She turned her thoughts to the present. "Watch it, you're about to miss the turnoff—" She pointed to the off-ramp that was quickly approaching.

Checking his right, Walker veered into the next lane, managing to get off just in time.

It was better for both of them if he changed the subject, he thought. "Why do you need to stop for a change of clothes?"

"This might take some time," she warned. She saw resistance in his eyes. "I really think you should pack a suitcase, too."

He shook his head. If he did, it would be like implying they had all the time in the world—when they didn't.

The thought gave him pause. He didn't used to be superstitious. But then, up until a short while ago, he hadn't believed something like clairvoyance was remotely possible.

"Whatever I need, I can buy."

"Must be nice," Eliza murmured, offering no other protest.

"Yes, I suppose it is. I always thought that money was really important, an end unto itself. I guess when you're poor, you feel that way." He brought the car to a stop at a red light. "But since I've gotten to this level, I really haven't had the time to enjoy the comforts that money brings."

"Maybe you should."

Walker looked at her and his eyes held hers for a moment. "Maybe I should."

The car directly behind them honked, dissolving the moment that shimmered between them.

Walker put his foot on the accelerator and drove.

* * *

Eliza swept into the reception area forty minutes later, nearly walking into Ben Underwood. Chad Andreini was close behind him. Both men were on their way out, and stopped when they saw Eliza.

Ben glanced at the overnight bag Eliza held in her hand. "Going somewhere?" His easy smile was enhanced with a touch of interest.

She shifted the bag to her other hand. "Laughlin."

Chad and Ben exchanged looks. In the short time she had been with the agency, no one had known her to take a day off. She could be found in the field or at her desk, seven days a week.

"Business or pleasure?" Chad asked.

The question made her think of Walker. Think of him in a way she knew he wouldn't appreciate, even though he'd been the one to kiss her, not the other way around. But she had kissed back. And felt something.

"Business," she answered crisply. "The pleasure comes in if I turn out to be right." She looked from one man to the other, glad she had run into them. They were essentially the reason she'd returned to the office. That, and to pick up a few of the electronic gadgets Megan loved so well. "You two still have connections with the police department?"

"Bedford's?" Chad guessed.

"Actually, I was hoping one of you knew someone who knew someone on the Laughlin police force."

Ben grinned, slipping a friendly arm around her.

To a person, they all felt very protective of Eliza at the agency. Though she was only slightly smaller than Megan, there was a vulnerability about her that Megan never displayed. Megan, they were all certain, could take care of herself no matter what. They weren't that sure about Eliza.

"Not directly," Ben told her. "But I've got a few friends who might know someone who knows someone."

He was teasing her, but she didn't mind. She welcomed it. "When you get to the end of the daisy chain, tell them that there's a possible kidnapping suspect in the Laughlin area—as well as his victim. If the facts check out, we're going to need backup."

"We?" Chad asked.

"Walker Banacek is coming with me. It's his daughter."

Ben nodded. They were all up on each other's case. "Leave it to me," he promised.

"Look out for yourself," Chad called after her as she began to walk into her office.

She looked over her shoulder quizzically. Chad was usually reserved. It had taken his wife, Veronica, to bring him around a little, but this was unlike even the new Chad. "What do you mean?"

Everyone had noticed a change in Eliza since she'd begun working on the Banacek case. A glow that hadn't been there before, despite all her natural gentle warmth.

He purposely left it vague. "Women aren't the only ones with intuition."

A kind of defensiveness rose within her, but she shrugged it away. Chad meant well. "They also aren't the only ones who can be wrong," she told him with an enigmatic smile. "I'll call in after we land to see if either of you came up with any names I can drop or use," she said with a wink.

Her smile faded a little as she closed her door behind her. Eliza leaned against it for a second. Her own reflection in the window caught her eye. What was it that Chad had seen that she wasn't seeing? Peering closer, she still didn't see it.

With a shrug, she dismissed Chad's comment as just so much talk.

Eliza had just enough time to tell Carrie and Savannah where she was going, leaving Carrie to fill Cade in. After packing a small combination fax, scanner and printer into her suitcase, she snapped the lid closed just as Walker came into her office, anxious to get started.

He picked up the suitcase from her desk for her, and a beat later the weight registered. Walker looked at it in surprise. "What have you got in here?"

"It's the suitcase of the millennium," she joked. Walking out, she led the way to the main door. "One change of clothes and enough hardware to set up my own office, no matter where I am."

Holding the door open for her, Walker thought of the farmhouse. "As long as there's electricity."

Amusement tugged on her mouth as she popped open her purse and displayed enough batteries to last a full night. "Prepared."

"Yes, it seems that you are." Reaching the elevator bank, he pressed the down button. His arm brushed against hers. "For anything."

She stole a side glance at him as a current rippled through her. *That* she wasn't sure about.

She could sense there was something wrong the moment they got into the elevator together. There was no one else there to distract her, and she could feel the discord flowing from him. She waited until they had left the building and were on their way to his car. Hers Carrie had promised to drive to her place. Savannah was going to drive her back to the lot so she could get her own VW.

"What's wrong?" she asked quietly, as he put her suitcase in the trunk. "Other than the obvious," she added.

Walker closed the trunk firmly. The word *nothing* hovered on his lips as he rounded the rear of the car and got in behind the wheel. But Eliza was too close to this, too close to his thoughts, to lie to. And maybe, just this once, talking would help him deal with what was going on inside. Not talking about it had never managed to help him any. It had just allowed the pain to fester.

The pain that was now coming to the forefront.

"She was only a few miles away. All this time,

packing her things away, burying her in my heart, she was only a few miles away. If—''

The word echoed in his head, looming large. Frustration chewed away at him. Walker looked at the woman he was putting all his faith into, faith he hadn't realized he had.

''That's the irony of it, isn't it? *If.* A tiny word that could change the course of history. My history. Bonnie's history. Rachel's,'' he added quietly. ''*If.* If only I had stayed home the day Bonnie was kidnapped, maybe Rachel wouldn't have gone to the store, or, at least, not taken Bonnie with her. If I had just done a few things differently... And once she was kidnapped, if only I had thought to...''

At that moment, she knew exactly what he was thinking. And it didn't do him any good to berate himself this way. ''To what?'' she challenged. ''To conduct a house-to-house search all through Bedford? You know that's not possible.''

''No, but I could have done something.''

''There wasn't anything to do,'' she insisted. ''Don't you see? You did everything you could. The FBI did everything they could.''

He didn't believe that, not anymore. Perhaps not even then. How could she? ''You found her, or, at least, where she'd been.''

''Only after she'd reached out to me,'' she reminded him.

He forgot what he was going to say an instant after it came to him. Instead, he was struck by the miracle

of the woman who had come to him. A miracle in so
many ways. "You really do see things, don't you?"

He wasn't challenging her, he was just talking out
loud, she thought. There was a difference. She began
to relax again. "Yes."

"What's it like? Really," he asked, wanting to
know, to understand. He had no frame of reference.
"I can't begin to imagine that kind of power."

"It's not a power—at least, not for me." Sometimes it was more of a curse, certainly a burden. And
it cost her. Isolating her from everything normal.
"I'm just a transmitter, nothing more."

"You're a hell of a lot more and you know it. At
least, you are to me. If you hadn't pushed—hadn't
kept after me to believe you—none of this would be
happening. Don't you see how special that makes
you?" Walker said.

"It doesn't make me special," she countered. "It
makes it my job. That's what I'm supposed to do as
'the messenger' or whatever you want to call my
function in all this. I'm supposed to shake people up
and make them listen. But my dreams, or the things
I 'see' aren't always so easy to interpret as the one
involving Bonnie turned out to be." She only wished
they were. That part of life might at least be less
difficult for her.

Looking at Walker, Eliza could see that he really
didn't understand. She decided to give him an ex-
ample. "I met Savannah because I had a dream about
a child I thought was her little girl. I saw the little

girl drowning in what I took to be a lake. I got in touch with her, and Savannah went through hell as the police dragged the lake, looking for her daughter. It turned out that the dream I had was about the daughter of the woman who had actually kidnapped Aimee. That was the little girl who drowned—and she'd drowned in a pool, not a lake. It all turned out to be connected, but not in a straightforward manner.''

He didn't know about her other cases and he didn't care, not right now. What concerned him was the case she was on now. His case. Bonnie's case.

''Well, this obviously was. And you were right. Those people must have kidnapped Bonnie to replace their own daughter.''

He was thinking positively. Maybe she had done a good job, after all. It was time she stopped feeling sorry for herself for whatever reason and concentrated on bringing this case to a proper conclusion.

''Looks that way, doesn't it? Now all we have to do is hope that we find them at this address.'' She took the piece of paper out of her purse and looked at it. ''Ben and Chad at the agency are both ex-policemen. Between the two of them, they have connections with the Laughlin police department. Ben promised he'd give the Laughlin P.D. a call, put them on the alert about a possible kidnapper in the area. If Wallace Allen and his wife are there and holding Bonnie, we can have the police moving in in a matter of minutes.''

He nodded grimly. "Sounds good to me."

She didn't like the way his hands unconsciously tightened on the wheel, but she said nothing.

"You're wasting your time."

Lowering his hand, Walker stopped pounding on the door marked #2D and turned to see a woman in a housecoat coming toward them. Her flip-flops slapped noisily across the concrete floor with each step she took. About to go down the stairs, she was carrying a bag of garbage.

"Are they out?" Walker asked.

"You could put it that way. They're more than out, they're gone. Skipped out owing me two weeks' back rent. 'Case you haven't figured it out, I'm the landlady. I felt sorry for them because of the little girl. A little beauty, that one, but always so sad." She shook her head, vaguely incredulous. "Can't see how something so perfect had a couple of parents like them. One worse than the other, if you ask me. Maybe the kid was adopted."

Walker thought his heart had stopped beating. "The little girl, what did she look like?" He pulled his wallet out of his pocket before she could answer, flipping to Bonnie's photograph.

The woman squinted, leaning in close. "Yeah, that's her," she declared, straightening. She looked from Walker to Eliza. "You friends of theirs?"

He was about to say no. Anticipating him, Eliza interjected. "Yes, we are. We're from San Francisco and trying to hook up with Wallace and Janie. Do you know where they went?''

The woman glared at Eliza. ''If you owed me money, would you tell me where you were going?''

This was beginning to wear on him. For every high, there were two lows. He wasn't sure how much more he could stand. ''Do you know where he worked?'' Walker pressed.

''Not off the top of my head, but he wrote it on the rental agreement. Wouldn't have rented them the unit if he didn't. Let me get rid of this, and I'll take you to the office and look it up for you.''

Eliza was already taking the sagging garbage bag from her. ''Why don't I do that for you, and you take him to your office?'' she suggested.

''Fine by me. Dumpster's around back.''

Eliza flashed Walker an encouraging look before hurrying down the stairs.

Thanks to the rental agreement, they discovered that Wallace Allen worked, or had worked, at a combination gas station and convenience store located just off one of the freeway exits. They lost no time in driving there.

The man who owned the place had nothing good to say about him. Allen had been quickly fired after the owner had found him making an unauthorized withdrawal from the cash register. He told Walker and Eliza that he had no idea where Allen was, and cared less.

"Don't need to keep track," he told them. "See enough of his kind every day."

Eliza thanked him and turned to leave.

At the end of his rope, Walker went out first without saying a word. He didn't realize that Eliza wasn't with him until he turned around to say something to her. Looking around, he saw that she'd stopped to talk to one of the men working in the small garage pit next to the convenience store.

Instead of calling to her, he doubled back, arriving in time to hear the mechanic in the navy-blue uniform say, "Yeah, I know where Wally went. Said he had some friend dealing at a casino in Reno. Was going to try to hook up with him and see about getting a job dealing. Not that he had the hands for it." The mechanic scoffed contemptuously. "Couldn't even hold a hand of cards right."

"Did he happen to mention which casino his friend worked in?" Eliza asked.

The man shook his head. He stopped shaking it when Walker produced a twenty and held it in front of him. Suddenly, his memory made a miraculous recovery. "Oh, yeah, I think he said Mount Olympus."

"Did he tell you what his friend's name was?" Eliza pressed.

The mechanic looked at Walker. When Walker took out another twenty, a name suddenly merged from the man's mouth. "Jack Stewart. Said they used to be friends back home in Yuma. That's where he was from, he said. Yuma. Hell, they fry eggs on the sidewalk there in the summer. Couldn't get me there except in a pine box.'' The mechanic put his hand out, looking at Walker expectantly. ''That Yuma thing wasn't a freebie, you know.''

Curbing his disdain at a man who doled out information about a reprehensible person for money, Walker handed him another ten, then took hold of Eliza's arm and ushered her out.

''We make a pretty good team,'' she said, getting back into the car.

Her comment, said with genuine feeling, took the edge off his anger. He looked at her for a moment before starting the car. That was what he had begun to think of them as, he realized. A team.

That was a dangerous way for his thoughts to go. He couldn't afford to get distracted.

And yet...

''I guess we do at that,'' he agreed quietly. He turned the key in the ignition. The car hummed to life.

She knew he was eager to get to Reno, but it wasn't a short little hop and it was getting late. ''You know, it's almost dark. Why don't we get a couple of rooms at a hotel and see about getting an early start in the morning?''

''I'm not tired,'' he snapped, then instantly regretted it. He owed her everything. ''I'll drive, you get some sleep.''

That was the last thing she was prepared to do. ''If

I let you drive, I might be in for the big sleep, and I'm not ready to cash in just yet.''

Lack of sleep interfered with his thinking. ''I could just go on alone from here.''

Stubborn to the end, she thought. ''You need me,'' she pointed out.

She was right, he thought, and he knew it. Just like she'd been right all along. He surrendered. ''All right, any particular hotel?''

''Just the kind with beds.''

''Sounds good to me,'' Walker commented. Perhaps too good, he realized.

Walker forced his mind on to other things, trying to forget the way Eliza had looked in her kitchen this morning after her bathrobe sash had come undone, the sunlight filtered through what there was of her nightgown. Highlighting her body.

He didn't have much luck.

Chapter 13

She couldn't sleep.

The hotel they had booked for the night was a little off the beaten path, so there was no noise outside her window to bother her. The room was cozy, tasteful in its decor, the bed comfortable.

None of it mattered.

She couldn't sleep. Her thoughts were restless. And there was a vague disquiet roaming over her, making her unable to find a place for herself, whether in the bed or in the room.

She'd given up trying to fall asleep half an hour ago. With her robe loosely wrapped around her, she had begun to prowl around her room.

The restlessness only grew.

It was as if she were waiting for something to happen, but she had no idea what.

Catching her reflection in the mirror over the bureau, she shook her head at the anticipation she saw in her face.

She knew something was coming. But she didn't know whether it was going to be good or not.

Maybe she would just get dressed and go out, she thought. Anything was better than just sitting here, feeling as if she were going to explode and not even knowing why.

Making up her mind, Eliza began to rummage through her purse for her pad. If she was going out, she needed to leave Walker a message on the off chance that he felt the need to talk to her in the middle of the night.

Right, like they were *both* crazy, she mocked herself. Setting the pad aside, she took off her robe, then her nightgown. She just needed to get out for a while.

Crossing to the closet where she'd hung her street clothes, she stopped dead. Eliza felt the door vibrating a half beat before knuckles had actually met wood. Grabbing her robe, she hastily put it on, knotting the sash at her waist.

Instead of calling out to ask who it was, she went to the door and opened it.

Walker had already dropped his raised hand to his side and was turning away, thinking better of the sudden, overwhelming impulse that had taken him from his room to her door.

Her appearance cut short his retreat.

"Ordinarily, I'd tell you you're supposed to ask

who it is before opening the door, but I figure you already knew,'' he said wryly.

She smiled. A sudden flash of intuition told her that this would never change between them. He was always going to be sparring with the fine points of what she could or couldn't do within the parameters that defined her life and her abilities.

"I had a hunch," she told him simply. Stepping back to admit Walker, she closed the door behind him. "It's much too early for the wake-up call, and I didn't order room service."

He looked at her.

Feeling like an idiot.

Part of him wanted to bolt for the door again, like some kind of wet-behind-the-ears kid. But a wet-behind-the-ears kid had the advantage of some general idea what he was all about and where he wanted to get to.

Walker, on the other hand, didn't have a clue. All bets were off since he'd begun this odyssey.

Bonnie should have been all that was on his mind. Bonnie and nothing else.

And yet, he found his thoughts straying, drifting toward Eliza. His mind asking questions he couldn't answer. Creating feelings he couldn't acknowledge.

God, but he was confused. Confused and yet needy for the sight of her.

Knowing he should walk out with some mumbled excuse, he remained where he was. Remained and bared a little of his soul to her. "Then maybe your hunch can tell me what I'm doing here at twelve-thirty in the morning.''

The vulnerability in his eyes touched her. Spoke to her. She had an overwhelming urge to put her arms around him and tell him it was going to be all right. She wanted him to do the same to her.

''That's easy. You can't sleep.''

He shook his head. ''Not good enough. I haven't been able to sleep before.'' Just as restless as she had been a moment earlier, he began to roam the room. Always keeping her in his line of vision, because she was the source of all this unrest he was feeling. ''Never needed anyone to hold my hand before.''

And that bothered him, she thought. A great deal. But there was no reason for that. ''Then you're making progress.''

When she smiled at him like that, he had trouble concentrating. All he could think about was tasting her mouth again.

''Am I?''

''I think so.'' The distance between them decreased. She was drawn by a magnetism she was unable to resist. ''It's important for people to reach out to each other, at least once in a while. It's what makes us human. Makes us able to cope.''

Her voice was drifting over him like a siren's song. ''And who is it that you reach out to, once in a while?'' he asked her quietly.

The sound of his voice surrounded her like a warm blanket, making her feel safe. Giving her a sense of security that had been absent for so long from her life.

Like a woman in a trance, she found herself inches away from him. Her body heating. "There was my great-aunt, but she's gone now."

"So you have no one." It wasn't quite a question, not yet an assumption.

She wanted to protest that she had friends, that the people she worked with were more than just people in an office to her. That they all genuinely cared about one another.

But not in the way she sensed he meant. That deep down, intimate kind of sharing that came in the wee hours of the morning when shadows loomed larger and insecurities threatened to swallow you up whole.

"No." The single word slid from her lips like a raindrop on the petal of a rose.

"I see."

There was an internal struggle going on, one that he was losing. This wasn't right. Wasn't right for either of them. He was taking advantage of her, giving in to the moment. Losing his mind.

And yet, his mind had never been clearer. He wanted her. Wanted her the way he couldn't remember ever wanting anyone else before.

"Eliza..."

"Yes," she whispered. Her eyes shone brightly, not with a question, but with agreement. With some deep, untapped joy that was hurtling to the surface.

"You do take away the need for conversation,"

Walker told her, his mouth curving as he took her into his arms.

But she wanted conversation; she wanted words to hold to her breast.

"No, talk to me," Eliza urged. "Say things to me. Things you want to say because you're feeling them." *Things I need to hear.* "I promise there will be no accounting in the morning, no promises to keep. Just for tonight, for now—"

He laid a finger to her lips, stopping the flow of words. Lyrical though the sound of her voice was to him, he didn't want to talk, not now. His needs, his desires, were more basic than that.

Her eyes were huge, lustrous. Looking into them, he felt himself falling.

Threading his fingers through her hair on both sides of her face, Walker turned her mouth up to his and kissed her. Kissed her the way he'd been longing to for the past three hours, ever since he'd left her door and had gone into his own room.

The way he'd longed to ever since he'd last kissed her.

One kiss was too much.

A thousand wouldn't be enough.

A fierce need seized him, and he had to struggle to keep it reined in, before it got out of hand and frightened them both. As gently as possible, Walker kissed her mouth over and over again, each kiss growing longer than the one before.

He could feel his heart hammering wildly as he

drew her into his arms, his hands slipping away from her face and winding around her small, compact body. Holding her against him.

Or was that her heart beating that way, pounding so hard it made him believe it was his own? He didn't know, didn't understand. Didn't care to unravel the puzzle. All he cared about was making love to this woman. *With* this woman.

If that made him reprehensible, to think of making love at a time like this, he'd deal with it all in the morning. Right now, Walker knew he was incapable of making sense of anything. His needs had consumed him to such a degree that everything else was just a heap of ashes to be sifted through.

Later.

This had been what was coming. The instant she'd seen Walker in her doorway, she'd known. This was why she'd been so restless, her body like a fine watch that was in danger of being over-wound. There were all these pent-up feelings, pent-up with no release in sight.

Until she had seen him.

Now she knew. This was what was meant to be. They were meant to be together. Perhaps not forever, perhaps not even in the morning, but for tonight, they were meant for one another.

She felt his fingers gliding along the edge of her robe, felt him parting the silken material until the cool air and his hot gaze found her. Eliza bit back a moan as he cupped her breasts, the gesture forcing apart her robe even more.

His hands began to roam along her body, not roughly but gently, as if he were afraid that she would shatter if he touched her the wrong way.

As if she wouldn't shatter if he didn't.

Eliza felt every part of her body quickening in moist anticipation. She dug her fingers into his biceps, glorying in his gentleness, in the feel of his skin moving along hers.

Her pulse raced, accelerating with each pass. Impatience took hold of her, and she began tugging at the edge of the sweater he'd thrown on, tugging until she'd succeeded in pulling it up over his head.

A fine mat of light hair covered pectorals that were finely sculpted. She splayed her fingers along them, her palms cupping him just as he had cupped her. Excitement grew.

"You work out," she murmured.

"Occasionally."

He nipped at her ear, and was rewarded with the feel of her body melting against his. Her breathing grew louder, more rapid. Matching his. The excitement that poured through his veins was unimaginable and refused to be harnessed.

Walker found he had little control over himself, over his destiny. Like a man caught up in a current of a river that was rushing out to sea. He gave up trying to fight it, to tame it, and just let himself enjoy the journey.

Her skin was like cream beneath his hands. Walker slipped the robe down her shoulders and off her arms, his body quickening at the splendid form he discovered beneath.

The thought that he should fall to his knees in worship occurred to him, as did the thought of making her his.

As if he could, a small voice mocked him.

For a little while, though, he could, he told himself. And that was all he asked for. A little while. Tomorrow was too far away to think of. He had only now, and he was going to make the most of it.

Walker lay her down on the bed, his mouth never leaving hers. His hand found her body. And he lost himself in her.

As she did in him.

Eliza wasn't an experienced lover. There had never been a parade of men in her life. For her, lovemaking had never been a casual thing, to be taken lightly. A commitment of the heart came before a commitment of the body. There had only been one other man in her life, and he had left her.

As would this one.

It wasn't her gift telling her, it was a vague feeling that for her, there would be no everlasting happiness. Her great-aunt had told her that because of her gift, she belonged to everyone.

And thus would belong to no single man.

But for an hour, a moment, she could have this,

and it would suffice for the moments when there was nothing but silence and memories.

Like a woman enflamed, Eliza met him touch for touch, gesture for gesture, embrace for embrace. As his hands and his mouth roamed her body, so did hers explore his. Until they were intimately familiar with every inch, every pleasure that there was to be given and received. Both with one another and themselves.

Worlds opened up. Things were learned. And everything else was shut away.

There was no awkwardness, and shyness had long since been burned away. In place of that there was ecstasy and extreme pleasure and a happiness that could only be felt, not described.

And when he came to her, slick with sweat and pulsing with desire, she was ready for him, her hips arching from the bed, yearning to receive him. To become one with Walker in body as she had already become one with him in spirit.

For however long it was to last, Eliza knew she had never made such a connection with anyone as she had with him.

Walker caught her chin in his hand.

"Look at me," he whispered. "I don't want to share you with your visions or anything else that's in your head. I want you for myself, if only for this moment."

Her eyes held his. "You already had me," she told him softly. "Before you ever walked in the door."

He didn't believe her, but he wanted to. And for now, he told himself, wanting to was enough.

Hands meeting hers, fingers entwining above her head, Walker lowered himself into her, the yearning quickening in his loins, demanding release. Sheathing himself, he slowly began the movement that would encompass them both. Slowly at first, then becoming faster and faster until there was no breath left within either of them.

Until there were no words, no walls, and no reality other than the two of them and this wondrous cloud they had happened upon strictly by chance.

And clung to by design.

As climax came to him, he felt Eliza shiver beneath him and knew that they had reached it together.

An incredible feeling of fulfillment came over him. Rather than give in to exhaustion, he tightened his arms around her and held her to him, comforted by the sensation of her heart beating against his.

She gave herself up to the feeling that was around her, to the afterglow of lovemaking, to the security of having his arms around her.

With all her heart, Eliza wished that just this once, she could freeze time. Because this was the moment that she would choose to freeze.

This was the moment she would always remember, no matter how old she grew to be.

Chapter 14

"Eliza."

Something in his voice made her stiffen, both inside and out. Closing her eyes, she sought for strength. She had thought she'd have a little more time before his regrets would begin forming.

But it was different for men, she knew. Once the act of lovemaking was completed, they went about the business of living, while women lingered on the memory and the feelings it invoked. For women, for her, life wasn't conducted like a business, straightforward and moving on, it was all about love and loving.

She'd known what she was up against before it had begun.

Trying to tell herself she was braced, Eliza opened

her eyes and turned toward him. His face was mere inches away from hers. Her pulse quickened just to look at him. "Yes?"

Walker slowly glided the back of his hand along her arm. The softness he found whispered things to him, making him want her even though he'd felt spent only a moment ago. There was so much he wanted to say to her; the words were becoming jumbled up in his mind, on his tongue. He'd never been any good at putting his feelings into words, or even at acknowledging his feelings.

Still, he had to try. "I didn't mean for this to happen."

Damn, why couldn't he have kept that to himself a little while longer? she wondered. It was the same thing he'd said to her when he'd first kissed her. She didn't need his confession, not yet, not now. Delving deeper, she forced herself to sound light.

"Don't worry, I'm off the meter. There's no extra charge for fraternizing."

He didn't understand the flippant answer. It was so unlike her. Uncomfortable, thinking better of the verbal blunder he'd almost made, Walker began to withdraw. Keeping his feelings to himself.

Then something stopped him.

It was the look in her eyes. A hurt look. She was hurt, and he had no idea why. All he could do was offer her the truth, and hope that somehow it would erase what he saw.

"But just because I didn't mean for it to happen

doesn't mean I regret that it did. I just regret that you might think I was taking advantage of the situation." He looked into her eyes and tried desperately to understand what she was thinking. "Of you."

She cupped his cheek, smiling softly. "It's not in you to take advantage."

He laughed shortly. She knew nothing about him. "That's where you're wrong." He thought of what someone had said of him recently. "I can be ruthless if I have to be."

He was talking about the man he was behind his office desk. She wasn't. She was talking about the inner man. "It's not in you," she repeated softly.

Walker looked into her eyes. Eliza made him think he was a better man than he perceived himself to be. He'd never thought of himself as evil, but he'd had to have been heartless to have allowed his wife to take all the blame for what had happened to Bonnie. So much so that she killed herself. Heartless. There was no other explanation for it.

He shook his head, sweeping her hair back away from her face. "I think that your clairvoyance is experiencing some technical difficulties."

She laughed at that. It was the first time she'd associated humor with her gift, the first time she'd heard a joke that had made her smile instead of wince.

Something warm and comfortable bloomed within her as she looked at Walker. "That only happens when I'm personally involved."

"Are you?" The question came of its own volition.

Given a chance, he wouldn't have asked. Not knowing created no obligations. And yet the question insisted on being asked. "Are you involved personally?"

There was no need for introspection, no need for her to hesitate. But there was a need to protect. Both him and herself. She didn't want Walker to think that he owed her anything for what had just happened. And because she knew that once the case was over, they would both go their separate ways, there was a need to protect her own feelings. Because they would be hurt.

"I think I'd better leave that unanswered."

He had no idea whether he'd just been put in his place, or rejected. Or just left high and dry. He did know that he cared for none of the above.

Male pride would have had him retreating, but there was something greater at stake than pride. What, he wasn't about to try to ascertain now. He didn't feel himself equal to it.

But he did want her.

"Just as well," Walker allowed, rising up on one elbow and bringing her closer against him. "We've already done too much talking, anyway." He brought his mouth down to hers.

Whatever protest was forming on her lips melted in the face of his renewed ardor.

As did she.

It astounded her that within the cauldron of her exhaustion there was an untapped vein of energy that surfaced and galvanized the instant he touched his mouth to hers. Threading her fingers through his thick hair, she kissed him back with passion and forgot to think about anything else except the way she felt when he made love with her.

The sun seemed to be painted in the sky, a stagnant red ball of fire. It was beating down mercilessly, threatening to fry everything in its path until it turned into something leathery and unrecognizable. Nothing moved save the small, navy-blue car. Years past its prime, it rattled and wheezed as, crammed with discord, it made its inharmonious way along the sparsely traveled road.

There were people in the car. Angry people. Unhappy people.

Three people.

A sign appeared on the right side of the road, growing larger and larger until its peeling letters were visible: Yuma 200 Mi.

The sign continued to grow larger even after the car had passed it. It seemed to fill every inch of space until there was nothing else but the sign visible. The sign and an oppressive heat.

And then there was a single, momentary flash of a face pressed against the rear window. The face of a sad child. Fading.

"No!"

Shaking, Eliza sat up, tears shimmering in eyes that were opened wide and unseeing.

Arms came up around her, trying to hold her. She fought to shrug out of the grasp.

He was going to keep her from getting away. She had to get away.

Struggling, she fisted her hands and began to beat at arms that wouldn't release her.

"Eliza, Eliza, it's me." Walker's voice came to her from leagues away. "What is it?"

A dream, she'd had a dream.

She tried to draw air back into her lungs, then sagged against Walker's chest like a rag doll whose batting had been pulled out, drained beyond belief.

Understanding none of it except that she needed to be comforted, to be held, Walker ran a gentling hand over her hair. It was damp, even though the room was cool. Murmuring soothing words, he began to slowly rock as he cradled her against him.

"It's okay, Eliza, it's okay. You're safe, here with me. You just had a bad dream, that's all. But you're safe now."

Safe. Eliza held on to his arm like a child caught in a riptide, clinging to the one branch that would keep her from going under. She forced herself to absorb the comfort, the words. To absorb the sensation of well-being that was usually so foreign to her.

These kinds of dreams were not uncommon for her. They burst upon her brain often enough. What was uncommon was to have someone there to hold her, to make her feel safe. To ground her and remind her that for her, there were two realities, and she couldn't allow the second to blot out the first.

When she finally caught her breath, Eliza said, "Allen isn't going to Reno."

Stunned, he stared at her. For one beat he stopped stroking her hair, and then forced himself to resume again. Her power, because that was what it was to him no matter what she chose to call it, made him uneasy. He didn't like not understanding. It made him feel as if he had no control whatsoever in the situation.

Walker didn't think to question how she knew. He just took it for granted that Eliza had had a sign within her dream. That was enough for him.

"Then where are they going?"

She saw the sign again, its letters looming large. "Yuma."

"Why?"

She raised her head and looked at him. His simple question created an answer within her that she hadn't been aware of until this moment.

"Because he's from there. Because he just found out that his mother died last week. He's going back because he's hoping to sell her things and get some money together."

Again, Walker didn't think to challenge her. It occurred to him that sometime in the past few days, he'd made a transformation. From nonbeliever to true believer, though he couldn't have said exactly when. All he knew was that he was placing all his faith in her visions, and thinking nothing of it.

They had to get on the road. Turning away, he slid to the edge of the bed, swinging his legs over. "How soon can you be ready to travel?"

"Five minutes. Ten if I'm trying to be neat."

He turned to look at her. Eliza had let the sheet drop from around her breasts. "Don't try." There was no time to do anything about the thoughts that sprang up in his mind unsummoned. His mouth took hers in a quick, rough kiss, and then he released her. "I like you tousled."

Walker was out of bed and hurrying into his clothes in another heartbeat, as was she.

Ten minutes later, they were on the road to Yuma, leaving behind them a bewildered clerk holding in his fist a large tip for managing to check them out so quickly.

It was only once they were in the car and Walker was behind the wheel again that he finally put the question to her that had been bothering him since he'd been jolted awake.

"You screamed 'No!' just before you woke up."

"Did I?" She shook her head. The memory wouldn't come. It was like hearing about someone else. "I don't remember doing that."

"You did. I was just wondering what would make you yell like that." He was almost afraid to ask. But he had to. If there was something terrible, he had to be prepared. "What did you see?"

"Their car getting farther and farther away." As she talked, she realized that there had been more people in her dream. That she and Walker had been in it, tiny figures on the sidelines. "Leaving us behind. I didn't want them to get away."

He looked at her before looking back on the road. "You actually saw them?"

No, she hadn't actually seen the couple in her dream. Instead, she had felt their presence. Would he scoff at that? She put it in as positive a reference as she could. "I saw their car. And I saw Bonnie looking out the back window. Looking at the road behind her. I think she was reaching out. I can't be sure. That's when I screamed. I didn't want her to get away."

He was trying very hard not to get completely carried away with all this. "You didn't happen to notice a license plate number, did you?" The fact that it would have been a license plate number that she had dreamed rather than seen didn't seem to dampen his fervor.

"No, but that can't be very hard to find out." Taking out her cell phone, she pressed the numbers to Savannah's line at the office, hoping she'd be in this early. She was. "Savannah, this is Eliza."

"Eliza, hi. How do you like Reno?"

"We're not in Reno. We think the suspect is en route to Yuma. The suspect's mother lived there. I want you to track down his car license for me, probably an Arizona issue, although it might be California.

He lived in Bedford for a while. Wallace Allen. A-l-l-e-n."

"Got it. I'll get back to you as soon as I can."

"I appreciate it." And then she thought of something. "And see if Ben or Chad know anyone who might be connected to the Yuma police department."

"Before or after I have my coffee?"

Eliza laughed. "After. I want you to be able to make out the numbers."

They picked up breakfast at a drive-thru. After a couple of bites, Eliza found she was too excited to eat. Walker, she noticed, seemed too nervous to have what he'd ordered, so the bag remained relatively untouched on the floor of the car. Neither one of them, though, passed on the coffee.

"Maybe we should have just ordered a gallon of coffee to go," she quipped. When her phone rang, she nearly spilled what was left in the container. She glanced at her watch. It had taken Savannah less than half an hour to get back to her; the woman was in a class by herself.

She answered the phone. "What did you find out?" she asked.

"That my eyes have trouble focusing before nine in the morning. I checked California with no luck. Allen never bothered changing his license while he was here. I've got a driver's license and car plates registered to a Wallace A. Allen in Yuma. Car's a 1985 Mustang. He's been dropped by several insurance companies. Your Mr. Allen is not the safest of drivers.''

Eliza decided not to pass the last bit of information on to Walker. He had enough on his mind as it was. ''Give me the numbers.'' She jotted both sets down as Savannah recited them. ''Great. Did you get a chance to talk to either Ben or Chad?''

''Chad's not in, but Ben thinks he might have someone for you.'' Savannah proceeded to give her the complex connection. ''Let me know if there's anything else.''

''Thanks. You're one in a million.''

''That's what I keep telling Sam. 'Bye.''

Eliza flipped her phone closed.

Walker had kept quiet as long as he could. ''Well? What did you find out?''

She passed the license plate numbers to him. ''Ben told Savannah he knows someone on the force who knows a detective Kane Madigan on the Bedford police department who in turn knows a detective Graham Redhawk on the Phoenix police force. He might know someone in Yuma.'' It was the long way around, but at least it gave them a possible in. ''We can get in contact with Redhawk, let him know what's going on and ask for his help.''

Had Walker not been in business, the amount of networking necessary to make a connection might have astounded him. As it was, he was grateful. Whatever it took to safely recover his daughter was fine with him.

He realized he was no longer thinking in terms of whether he would find her, but whether he could get her back unharmed. It was a good feeling.

"The police force sounds like one great big fraternal club," he said.

She thought of Chad and Ben, and of several other police officers she knew personally. "I guess we can be grateful for that. According to what Ben knows, Detective Redhawk has a personal thing about anyone who'd kidnapped children. Ben already set the wheels in motion and called him. He assured Savannah that Redhawk will be more than happy to cooperate and do anything we need. On the record and off."

"Sounds like a good man to have in our corner." The reality of the situation suddenly rose up to grip him by the throat. For a single moment, Walker found himself almost unable to believe it. He glanced at Eliza. "Is it really going to happen? After all this time, am I really going to finally hold my daughter again?"

The emotion she heard in his voice brought tears to her eyes. The dreams, the nightmares, being isolated—it was all worth it to be able to help bring about this kind of a miracle.

"I gave you my word, didn't I?"

"Yes, you did." Reaching over, he squeezed her hand. "But you're not God."

She smiled at that, remembering the way her great-aunt used to refer to her ability as a God-given gift. "No, I'm not. Just consider me His helper."

* * *

The drive to Yuma was taxing, but they made good time. They drove as quickly as they could, exceeding speed limits when the road was open. To facilitate matters, and because Eliza felt they needed a base of operations should finding Allen take some time, she and Walker checked into a hotel as soon as they arrived in Yuma.

"Will that be one room or two?" the clerk behind the registration desk asked.

Walker spared Eliza a look, then made a judgment call. "One." He raised his brow as he looked at her again. Maybe he had assumed too much. He didn't want to pressure her. "Unless you'd rather—"

"One's fine," she assured him. She knew she had only a limited amount of time to savor being with Walker and she was going to do exactly that.

The bellhop who insisted on accompanying them to their room talked nonstop, wanting to know if they were on vacation and what had brought them to Yuma. Once inside, he deposited Eliza's suitcase, opened the drapes, and gave all indications that he was going to become their own personal guide.

Walker took out a twenty and held it out to him, making sure he was standing by the door when he did so. The bellhop took the cue and the money. Quiet was restored within the room.

"Nice trick," Eliza commented, kicking off her high heels.

She did that whenever she planned to remain in a

room. It was a habit she had, he noticed, surprised at the way he picked up on the small things that made her what she was, even at a time like this.

"I learned a long time ago," he told her, "that most annoyances and problems go away if you just throw money at them."

"I wouldn't know." She'd never had much money to throw.

Eliza sat down on the bed, pulling the telephone to her.

He leaned against the bureau, watching her, too restless to sit. "Calling Redhawk?"

She nodded, taking out the number Ben had given to Savannah.

Graham Redhawk was waiting for her call. On the Phoenix police force, he had access to the Arizona police force's infrastructure, and placed it all at Eliza's disposal. Everyone in the department considered recovering a missing child safely the most rewarding experience of all.

"Do you have a license number for the car?" he asked.

She gave it to him, along with Allen's driver's license information. "I don't know where his mother's house is in Yuma," she began.

"No problem," Graham assured her. "The answer's just a phone call away."

Eliza paused for a moment. She didn't know Redhawk and didn't know how he might take her request.

"The girl's father and I need to check it out ourselves before anyone actually gets involved."

"That could prove to be pretty risky. You don't know who you're dealing with—"

"But I do," she interrupted. "I have an entire psychological profile on the man." She knew Allen, she felt, probably better than his wife, certainly better than his great-uncle.

"The real thing tends to be a lot more dangerous than something written down on a piece of paper, Ms. Eldridge," Graham told her amicably.

She understood his reasoning, but she had hers, as well. "We're aware of that, which is why we want the police for backup. But I don't want to stir up everyone on the outside chance that this doesn't pan out."

"Understood. Why don't you let me make a few preliminary phone calls," Graham suggested, "and then I'll get back to you."

It was a compromise. She agreed that they would wait in the hotel for Redhawk's return call.

When she hung up, she saw a look she couldn't interpret in Walker's eyes. "What?"

The expression *So near and yet so far* had occurred to him more than once on the drive to Yuma, undermining his newfound faith. Hearing her just now only added to that uneasiness.

"What did you mean just now, 'on the outside chance that this doesn't pan out'? I thought you were convinced you were right."

How did she put this without losing him? "I am convinced—but I'm also human."

His eyes narrowed. Was she going to go back on what she'd told him? "Meaning?"

"Meaning, I'm fallible. Maybe I am interpreting this wrong, maybe I missed something. Maybe—" She blew out a breath, dragging her hand through her hair, feeling frustrated.

"I would have thought that you'd built up more faith in yourself than this," Walker said.

"Ordinarily, so would I." She shook her head, turning away. "Maybe I want this too much." She pressed her lips together. "Sometimes I get in my own way."

He came up behind her, placing his hands on her shoulders. "I haven't seen you trip yet."

Chapter 15

"Are you sure this was his mother's property?" Walker asked the tall, gregarious man who had led the way into the small, crammed house that smelled of death and neglect. The afternoon sun remained standing just outside the doorway, refusing to enter.

The homicide police detective whom Graham Redhawk had gotten in contact with on the Yuma police force, Buddy Bear, was also a member in good standing of the Navajo tribe and a personal friend of Graham's. He'd bent the rules slightly and accompanied them here, after having familiarized himself not with their case, but with the woman to whom the house was still deeded.

"Still is, according to the country records, until the paperwork goes through. Maude Allen's only living direct descendent is Wallace Allen, whereabouts presently unknown," Buddy recited. He passed the Stetson he'd removed on entry from hand to hand. "There're some distant cousins and such, but nobody seems to know where they are, either. If Maude's friend hadn't come looking for her, no telling how long that poor lady would have gone undiscovered, lying in her bed like that."

Walker looked around, his frustration mounting. He realized that Eliza wasn't in the living room with them. "Eliza?"

"In here."

Her voice was coming from the rear of the small house. Hoping she'd discovered something, Walker made his way to the back. He found her in the bedroom, her hands on the sheets where, a little more than a week ago, Maude Allen had been discovered.

A feeling of discord had met her when they'd walked into the living room, but as far as Eliza could determine, it didn't seem to reach into this room.

Eliza looked at Walker as he entered. "She died peacefully," she murmured. "In her sleep."

He knew it was callous of him, but right now he wasn't interested in the passing of a woman he didn't know, only in the whereabouts of her son. The son who was holding his daughter prisoner.

"Where is he, Eliza? Has he been here?"

She shook her head, answering his last question first. "No."

"Neighbor said she hadn't seen the son around for

over two years," Buddy informed them. "Not since
the little girl died."

Walker felt the knife rake across his heart. He
looked at the other man sharply. "What little girl?"

"The granddaughter." The detective looked over
toward the opposite wall where a massive bureau
stood. It appeared completely out of place in the room
full of cheap furniture. "Mousy little thing, like her
mother." He crossed to the bureau where dust and
photographs dressed in dime-store wooden frames
had collected. "This is her." He held up a photograph, obviously taken in front of the house. It represented three generations of Allen women. "One
sadder looking than the last, if you ask me."

Eliza took the frame from him and looked at the
child. She appeared to be the same age and general
coloring as Bonnie had been at the time of her kidnapping. But the police detective was right; there was
a sadness to the little girl, a sadness that wasn't evident in any of the photographs she'd seen of Bonnie.

She handed the frame to Walker. "What happened
to the little girl?" she asked Buddy.

"We never did get the straight of it," he confessed.
"Girl's father claimed he woke up one morning to
find her in her bed, not breathing. Said she'd taken a
bad fall from the swing the day before."

Eliza could see that the detective had his doubts
about the truth of the story. He was moving his fingers
around the edge of his hat again.

"They buried her before anyone even knew she

was dead. I came around to ask him a few questions, but he was already gone. Took off with his wife. Maude wouldn't say anything against him.''

Walker's frown deepened. He didn't like the sound of this. If Allen *had* killed his own little girl for some reason, how would the man treat Bonnie? He'd allowed himself to be placated by the thought that whoever had taken her was desperate to replace a lost child and therefore would love his daughter and treat her well. But if they'd killed the first child, then Bonnie could be in imminent danger.

"Did you exhume the body?" Walker asked.

Buddy shook his head. "Maude said he had the little girl cremated."

Eliza shivered, running her hands over her arms. The image of a little girl being lowered into a grave ricocheted through her brain. The room darkened even more, finally disappearing altogether.

She heard Wallace yelling.

"Damn it, I ain't drunk no more. Let me outta this place. Get my wife to bail me out and get me outta here, you hear me?"

"Eliza?"

The scene broke apart into a million pieces. Blinking, she focused as light began filling in the spaces. She saw the concerned look on Walker's face. Eliza took a deep breath to steady herself.

"Allen's in jail. Or was. I'm not sure." She looked at Walker apologetically, wishing she could be more help. "But he hasn't gotten here yet."

"In jail?" The first thing he thought of was Bonnie. Had Allen harmed her? Was she all right? "Why? What's he done?"

Steepling her fingers before her, Eliza covered her face with her hands, trying to summon a thought, a feeling. Something. Only fragments came.

"Drunk and disorderly. A fight." She looked at Walker. "I don't know where or with whom, but it isn't anything major."

He wasn't satisfied. Walker gripped her wrist. "And Bonnie?"

"Nothing." She saw the stricken look on his face. "No, that's good. If anything had happened to her, I would have felt it."

Nerves frayed, exhausted from the emotional roller coaster he kept boarding, only to be disappointed at the end of each ride, he challenged her. "How do you know that? How do you know for sure? You said yourself that your 'channels' are down most of the time."

She knew his anger wasn't really directed at her, but it stung, anyway. "I just know. I can't put it any plainer than that, not even for myself. I just know."

Eliza became aware that the tall police detective had been silently taking in this exchange. She flushed. "I—"

Buddy held up a hand. "No need to explain. Gray told me all about it. I grew up listening to the elders repeat legends about people like you."

She ran a hand through her hair, feeling just as

frustrated as Walker. "I'm not exactly the stuff that legends are made of."

It was suddenly too close for her in the small bedroom. The walls felt as if they were closing in. Eliza walked out, searching for something that might trigger another connection for her.

But nothing came.

Turning on her heel, she discovered that Buddy had followed her.

"Can you put out an APB on Allen's car? He is a kidnapping suspect," she added, in case there was some argument against doing so.

Buddy hooked his thumbs into the belt loops of his jeans. "We can't do it officially because of some legal red tape about initial jurisdiction, but let me put some feelers out and see what I can do." Taking out his cell phone, he turned away to make his calls.

"And in the meantime, we wait," Walker said in disgust, coming up behind her.

She could feel his frustration. "There isn't anything else we can do."

She was right and he knew it. Knew that he was being unfair to her, that she was doing everything she could. That she had managed to get him farther than the FBI had when they were handling the case.

He didn't do apologies well, but she deserved one. "Look, I'm sorry I lost it back there. I didn't mean to take it out on you."

All it took was one "I'm sorry" and the hurt feelings melted away. She didn't want him to dwell on it. "Don't worry about it. Like I told you, that kind of thing doesn't faze me. My father was a lot better at it than you in his day."

"Who did he take things out on?" He placed his hand on her shoulder, forcing her to look at him. "You?"

She shrugged. She shouldn't have said anything. All it did was dig things up that were best left alone. "It was hard on him, having a spook for a daughter. And I don't think he ever really forgave himself for not believing me."

The two didn't seem to go together. "Forgave himself?"

She didn't like retelling the story, didn't like reliving it. But Walker needed to be comforted and distracted, so, for his sake, she opened up old wounds that had never managed to heal.

Eliza stared straight ahead at the peeling wallpaper in the faded living room. "I had a premonition about my mother's death. Actually, I guess it was a vision." The label didn't matter. The result was the same. "I saw her at home, choking on an almond she'd accidentally inhaled. My father and I were away from the house at the time, getting something from the hardware store—my mother had made him take me with him, hoping that spending time together might make him feel closer to me."

If only she'd known before she left, she would never have gone. But she couldn't control things like that. They controlled her.

"I knew something was wrong even before the vision actually came. I pleaded with my father to hurry back, that she was choking, but he got so angry at me for making a scene that he hit me. Not hard," she added quickly, seeing the look on Walker's face. "He just didn't know how to make me stop. He finally left everything in the store and took me home, saying my mother would know what to do with me. When we got there, she was dead. He went all to pieces." She looked at Walker, her expression softening. "He really did love her a great deal. It was hard for him to look at me after that."

He wanted to hold her, but he wasn't sure if he should. "But you'd tried to get him to go home."

She nodded. "Exactly. And looking at me reminded him that he hadn't listened. That if he had…" There was no point in repeating the obvious. The past couldn't be changed no matter how often it was relived in memory. "Like I said, you're a piker."

"Good news," Buddy told them, pocketing his phone as he came back into the room. "The car was already spotted. A car matching the description you gave us was used in a getaway after a convenience store robbery. Someone got a partial number plate down—the numbers match Allen's Mustang."

Walker didn't see it as good news. "If he robbed a store, he could go anywhere."

"He'll come here." With each word Eliza uttered, she felt more certain. "It's his home base. He doesn't think anyone knows who he is or where he's from.

He'll come here," she repeated with certainty. "Where and when did the robbery occur?"

"An hour ago," Buddy told her. "Just outside of Carson City."

"Carson City." The details jibed. She did a quick calculation in her head. "That means, unless he drives straight through, he'll probably be here in the morning."

Buddy glanced at his watch. It was three in the afternoon now. "I get off duty at eight. I can be here within the half-hour, watch the house. I'll give you a call if Allen shows up."

"Oh, he'll show all right," Eliza promised him.

The police detective seemed to be forgetting one thing, Walker thought. He was the father. "Shouldn't we be the ones—?"

The look on the other man's face was understanding and, he was soft-spoken as he made his point. "If I do it, it's unofficial police business. If you do it and anyone sees you, it could be taken as stalking, or harassment—" He directed his attention toward Eliza. "In case you're wrong."

"She's not wrong."

The certainty in Walker's voice had Eliza looking at him in surprise. The fence he'd been sitting on had come down. For a moment, she was speechless.

"Okay, then keep your phones open." Buddy led the way out of the house, shutting the door behind Eliza. The lock clicked into place. "I'll be calling you. For now, why don't the two of you go back to the hotel and get something to eat? Rest if you can.''

Eliza exchanged looks with Walker. They were both thinking the same thing: *Easier said than done.*

"I think we'll just stick around in the vicinity, in case Allen makes better time than we anticipate," Walker told him.

The detective began to protest, then thought better of it. "Fair enough. Anyone asks, you never said anything to me. I'll be back by eight-thirty."

"I never realized sitting in one place could be so tiring." Walking into the hotel room five hours later, Walker dropped the entry card onto the bureau. Every bone in his body felt stiff.

"It's not the sitting, it's the anticipating that does it."

Following him in, Eliza rotated her shoulders as she spoke. She took out her cell phone, placed it on the bureau in plain sight. If Buddy called, she didn't want to waste precious seconds hunting for it in her purse.

Empathy had her touching Walker's shoulder. He was going through hell, and there was nothing she could do to shorten his stint. "It'll be over soon."

He covered her hand with his own, knowing she only meant to comfort him. There was still part of him that doubted, part of him that felt he was forever doomed to this limbo he'd already resided in for two

endless years. Bringing her hand to his lips, he kissed
it.

"I just want you to know that if it's not, I don't
blame you."

There was kindness in his eyes, kindness that managed to transcend the layers she always kept wrapped
around her heart. Armor plating turned to gauze and
then slipped away entirely.

She cupped his cheek with her hand. Moving his
head, he pressed a kiss to her palm.

She saw him then, saw him not as he was this moment, but as he would be. Making love to a woman.
To her. The flash left her warm. And yearning.

Raising his head, he saw the look in her eyes.
"You're seeing something again, aren't you?"

She nodded. "I think so."

She was usually more certain than that, he thought.
"Think so?"

Her eyes met his. "It's you."

He saw a shyness there. A shyness he found irresistible. It made him want to protect her and possess
her at the same time.

"What am I doing?"

Eliza ran the tip of her tongue over her lips. "Making love."

His mouth curved. "To anyone we know?"

She took a deep breath before answering. "To me.
I don't know if that qualifies as anyone you know."
She looked away for a moment, feeling suddenly lost.

"I don't even know if that qualifies as anyone I know."

He raised her chin so that their eyes met again. The look in his held her fast.

"The way to get to know something," he told her softly, slowly unbuttoning her blouse, "is to go over it. Very, very slowly." He parted the open blouse, coaxing it from her shoulders. "Until you know it like the back of your hand." He pressed a kiss to her bare shoulder and felt her involuntary shiver against him. It heightened his excitement. He needed her softness to see him through the night. "Better than the back of your hand." He moved the fabric from her arms. The blouse drifted to the rug, discarded, forgotten.

Her heart was already hammering wildly. Anticipation raced through her body, singing. "And when is this exploration going to take place?"

"No time like the present."

Her emotions were close to the surface. They always were after she experienced an episode of seeing. It made her vulnerable and an easy prey. Because she knew the state she fell into, Eliza had learned how to put up defenses around herself.

But she didn't want those defenses up now, not against Walker. She didn't think they would go up even if she tried to resurrect them. There was something about Walker that broke through to her, that touched the inner woman she was, the one she'd kept hidden for so long. For he had given her what she wanted most. Respect. Compassion. And in return, she gave him herself. It was the greatest gift she had to offer, and she gave it willingly.

They undressed one another quickly, a sense of urgency permeating the very air they breathed. Hands raced over bodies, to be followed by questing lips. They sought to pleasure each other, while seeking sanctuary for themselves.

She shivered when his breath touched her skin, loving the sensation, the waves of anticipation that were created in its wake.

The feeling that this was meant to be, that she was home, did not leave her even at the height of her excitement.

Her fingers slid along the hard muscles of his back, gliding lightly, possessively over them. What would it be like to love a man and know that it was for all time? To feel safe in the knowledge that she had found her soul mate?

If that sensation, that feeling was ever attainable, it would feel like this, she thought. And it would be wonderful.

What was this spell she cast over him? Walker thought. Making him want her in the midst of emotional turmoil. In the years that had followed Bonnie's disappearance, he'd never wanted to be with a woman. It was as if that part of him, that need, had just been cut out. Had ceased to exist.

Yet here he was now, at the very edge of possibly, just possibly, finding his daughter again, and he was

discovering that his appetite had not only returned—
for it had never been a dominant force in his life—
but had grown more than tenfold.

He could not remember ever wanting a woman this
way, ever feeling about a woman the way he felt
about Eliza, not even during the years when sex was
all that there was supposed to be for an adolescent
boy.

Was she a witch, after all? Had she bewitched him,
made him act against his very nature?

He didn't know, wasn't sure, didn't even really
care. Not right now. For all that could be pushed to
the back of his mind. All he wanted now was fulfillment.

And to fulfill. Because her pleasure, her response,
was even more important to him than his own.

Grazing her body with ravenous, open-mouthed
kisses, he reveled in the way her belly quivered as he
passed his lips over it, found joy in the way her body
tensed, then slackened, as he brought her from one
peak to another with gentle strokes of his fingers
along the most sensitive part of her.

Unable to hold back, wanting her more than he
would ever have thought humanly possible, even
more than he had the first time they had been together, Walker joined his mouth to hers.

Then, very slowly, he slid into her to complete the
circle so that two could become one. Kissing her over
and over again, he began to move, first slowly, then
with more and more fervor.

He tasted her moan in his mouth, felt her surrender against his body. Urgency hummed within him, increasing the rhythm of his movements, until finally, a fiery, incredible release seized him, holding him fast until he was spent. Exhausted, he moved to one side, secure in the knowledge that she had completed the journey with him. Secure, for the moment, that she was here and she was his.

Kissing the top of her head, he cradled her against him and murmured her name as a blissful euphoria descended over him. He felt her mouth curve against his chest and felt the imprint of her smile as it branded him.

And slowly seeped into his soul.

Chapter 16

He was just beginning to fall asleep when the ringing jarred apart the contented feeling he'd managed so carefully. Immediately awake, Walker sat up, curbing the urge to grab the cell phone himself. He nudged Eliza needlessly—she was already awake.

"Your cell phone's ringing."

Rising up on her elbows, she cocked her head. Just as she thought, the ring was different. "No, the sound's not quite the same. It's yours."

Disappointment sent the emotional roller coaster he was doomed to ride on barreling down another incline. Getting out of bed, leaving behind the sheet for Eliza to cover herself with, he was naked as he crossed quickly to the bureau.

In no mood to talk, he flipped open the phone. "Hello?"

There was a momentary pause. "Walker?"

Trying to rein in his impatience, he still bit the word off. "Yes?"

"It's Jason. I know it's late, but I haven't heard from you in almost two weeks. What's going on? Where are you? Have you—?"

"You ask more questions than a reporter." Walker rubbed his jaw, feeling bad now that he'd snapped his greeting. Maybe he should have called Jason, but he'd been so wrapped up in finding Bonnie that everything else, including his business, had taken a distant backseat.

"I'm in Yuma."

"Yuma?" Walker heard a frustrated sigh on the other end. "Was I wrong? Is that clairvoyant leading you around on a wild-goose chase?"

"No, I don't think you were wrong." He glanced over his shoulder at Eliza. Sitting up, she had the sheet tucked around her breasts and was listening to every word. He found himself wanting her all over again, despite the spent condition of his body. "And she's not."

"Then have you…?"

Walker didn't want to say anything, didn't want to put it into words for the other man, in case he jinxed it. Until two weeks ago, he wouldn't have believed in jinxes and luck, but being with Eliza had opened up a whole other world for him, one that went beyond the dimension he knew.

Guardedly, he said, "I think we're about to."

"You're kidding." The enthusiasm in Jason's voice was boundless. "That's great. Where? How?" Jason paused, as if regrouping. "Look, I know it's late, I'll let you go. But call me first thing in the morning with details."

"I will," Walker promised, hoping he would remember to keep the promise.

"And Walker," Jason interjected just as Walker was about to disconnect the call, "if you need anything…"

Walker smiled. The rest wasn't necessary to put into words. "Yeah, I know. Thanks. I'll call you in the morning."

With that, he flipped the phone shut and placed it back on the bureau.

"She's not what?" Eliza asked the moment Walker came back to bed.

Keeping her mind on the conversation was the only way she could remotely keep her mind off the fact that Walker Banacek had to have one of the most gorgeous bodies she had ever seen, much less fantasized about. He looked at her quizzically as he got into bed next to her.

"When you were talking, you said, 'She's not.'" Instinct told her he hadn't been talking about Bonnie at that moment. "She's not what?" she repeated.

"Taking me for a ride." Leaning back against the headboard, he slipped his arm around her shoulders, drawing her close to him. Trying to recapture a frag-

ment of the euphoria he'd surrendered at the first ring
of his cell phone. "That was Jason."

"Yes, I know. I figured it out," she added when
he looked at her with one eyebrow raised in silent
speculation.

He smiled, enjoying the feel of her against him.
Wanting her again. "And how did you do that?"

"Your voice was softer."

He drew his head back to look at her, surprised by
the observation.

"When you're comfortable, the edge goes off your
voice. You're not comfortable with too many people," she added.

"No," he agreed, tilting her chin back so that he
could kiss her. "I'm not." But she wasn't among that
number. Instead, she belonged to the far smaller circle
of people he was comfortable with. Comfortable
enough with her not to be on guard about every word.
Comfortable enough with her to feel.

The stillness was broken by the sound of the cell
phone ringing again.

With an exasperated huff, Walker looked toward
the bureau. Jason must have forgotten something, or
maybe had grown too impatient to wait until morning
to be filled in.

Shifting, Walker started to get up. "I swear, if
that's Jason again—"

"No, this time it's my cell phone."

A premonition descended over her as she tugged

the sheet loose from the covers and away from the bed.

It was Buddy, she could feel it.

Draping the sheet around her quickly, she hurried to the bureau and picked up the smaller of the two cell phones. "Hello?"

Detective Bear's easygoing voice filled the receiver. "I'm giving you a heads-up, Ms. Eldridge. An '85 Mustang belonging to our boy is just pulling up into the driveway even as I'm talking to you."

Every nerve ending tightened. She dug her elbows into her waist to keep the sheet from falling as she held the cell phone with both hands.

"Is she with him?" Out of the corner of her eye, she saw that her question had nailed Walker's attention. He was on his feet instantly, coming toward her.

Eliza tilted the phone away from her ear a fraction, so that he could hear.

"There's a woman with him and a little girl," Buddy told her. "I'm calling for backup."

Something told her not to let him, not yet. She didn't know if it was a premonition, or just her own desire to get there first.

"Hold off for a few minutes—unless it's absolutely necessary," she qualified. It was a gamble, but she wanted to be there with Walker first, to find a way to get the little girl away without incident. "We'll be right there."

Walker had left her side. When she turned around, flipping the phone closed, she saw that he had already hurried into his clothes. She quickly followed suit. Neither spoke to the other, as if words would somehow break the spell.

Five minutes later, they were out the door and in the car.

Walker drove. They arrived fifteen minutes later, after flying down streets that had slipped into slumber hours ago. A thousand thoughts crowded through Walker's mind until he finally pulled up behind Buddy's car.

There were two lights on in the front of the house that sat across the street. Buddy's unmarked vehicle looked dark as they approached it. At first, it seemed empty, but drawing closer, Eliza saw that the detective had purposely slid down in his seat, so as to continue watching the front of the house without being seen himself.

Seeing them, Buddy sat up and got out of the vehicle. He ran one hand along his spine, but made no complaint. "Unless they went out the back way, they're still in there." Dark eyes looked from Eliza to Walker, as if to read their faces. "Look, I want no heroics." He turned to reach into his car. "I'm going to call for backup."

She had seen what too many police on the scene could do, been witness to the confusion that could erupt. Her main concern was the effect that kind of chaos would have on Bonnie. The child was already traumatized. She knew that for a fact.

Eliza caught Buddy's arm, stopping him. "Wait, let me try something." Both men looked at her quizzically. On the drive over, she had remembered something Savannah had told her that Sam used to gain access to a potential kidnapper's house. "I'll knock on the door, tell them I broke down just down the block and ask if I can use the telephone."

Buddy shook his head. "Too dangerous."

"I'll keep my cell phone open so you'll know the moment I see Bonnie," she pleaded. "Once I have her, you can come in. We need to make sure Bonnie's safe."

"Good plan," Walker agreed. "Only, I'll be the one going in with the open cell phone." He saw Eliza opening her mouth to protest, but he wouldn't let her talk. "I don't want you risking yourself. That's not a stable man in there."

She couldn't let him be the one to go in. "If Bonnie's in the room, she'll know you. And they featured your picture in the paper. Even if Bonnie's not in the room, Allen will probably recognize you."

She looked at the house. The sense of urgency was back. Bonnie was in danger, she was certain of it. Allen's temper was raw after the jail stint and the robbery. There was no telling what he could do if Bonnie made him angry. "My way's the only way to go, and we're wasting time talking. Don't worry," she told Walker, "I know what I'm doing. I've had training."

Up until this point, he'd only thought of her as

being a clairvoyant. He'd forgotten all about the fact that she was also a private investigator and had probably been schooled in self-defense.

But he still didn't have to like this. "All right, we'll do it your way."

Two minutes later, with Walker watching from Buddy's car, the police detective positioned at the rear of the house, and her cell phone opened and set to conference call so that both men could hear her, Eliza walked up the front steps of the house. Mentally counting to three, she knocked on the door.

She knocked three times before there was finally a response.

The door was yanked open. "Yeah, what do you want?" The abrupt tone shifted immediately as Wallace Allen took a look at the woman who was knocking on his door. His angry expression melted into a leer. "Well, what is it I can do for you, little lady?"

Fluffy, think fluffy, Eliza schooled herself, invoking every lightweight *femme fatale* she had ever seen in old, grade-B movies.

The look she gave Allen was a simpering one. "My car broke down just down the block. I saw your lights," she told him breathlessly. "Could I please use your phone to call a tow truck?"

He began to step back, then stopped. "Why'd you pick my house?"

She let her shoulders rise and fall, doing her best to seem lost and vulnerable. The type, she knew, that

Allen gravitated toward, the type that made him feel big and important.

The kind he liked to overpower. "I don't know, I just picked one."

He looked at her grudgingly, then finally shrugged. "Okay, c'mon in." He closed the door behind her.

The atmosphere had changed within the room since she'd been here earlier today. Now there was an oppressive feel of evil permeating it. She didn't have to look far to know where it was coming from.

Looking at him, she purposely bit her lower lip. The hungry look he gave her made her flesh crawl. "I'll only be a minute. Where's your phone?"

"In the kitchen." But as she began to walk in the direction he pointed, Allen grabbed her arm. "But what's your hurry, honey? Maybe you want to stay a while and talk."

"Who's there, Wallace?"

At the sound of his wife's voice, Allen's expression instantly turned malevolent. "Get back to your room, Janie," he snapped.

At that moment, Bonnie ran into the room, stopping short just in front of Eliza. She looked terrified.

"Is this your daughter?" Eliza kept her voice casual as she moved toward the girl. Bonnie looked up at her and their eyes locked. Again, Eliza felt some sort of connection. She smiled brightly at the girl. "Hi, what's your name?"

"Bonnie." She said the name firmly.

"It's Miranda," the bedraggled woman who had

looked in a second ago insisted. Coming up behind Bonnie, Janie Allen clamped her hands down on each small shoulder, pulling the girl against her. Licking her lips nervously, she told Eliza, "She just made up that other one."

Subtly, Eliza moved nearer. "Bonnie, Miranda—they're both pretty names." Her eyes remained on Bonnie's. She kept her voice soft, friendly. "I used to have a pretend name, too. Mine was Princess Moonflower."

The next moment, both the front and back doors were rammed open, slamming against the opposite walls. The sounds ricocheted through the house, making it shudder. Walker came flying at Allen.

"What the…?" The curse on Allen's tongue never emerged as his face met Walker's fist. Wallace Allen went down instantly, knocked out from the dead-on force of the blow.

Screaming, his wife tried to grab Bonnie and run, but Eliza wrapped her arms around the little girl and pulled her quickly toward her. She turned her body so that it shielded Bonnie.

"Give her to me, give her to me! I can't lose her twice. I can't! Please, give me my baby!" Shrieking, wailing, Janie fell to her knees as Buddy slipped handcuffs on her.

"You have the right to remain silent—and I really wish you would," Buddy interjected before continuing with the familiar words. "If you wave this right…"

"Got an extra pair of those things?" Walker asked, standing guard over Allen. The other man was out cold on the floor, but they all knew he could wake up at any moment.

Reaching into the back pocket of his jeans, Buddy threw the handcuffs to Walker. "I had a hunch we might need them."

Quickly cuffing Allen, Walker rose. He looked at his daughter. Eliza was holding the little girl in her arms. He crossed to them on shaky legs.

He'd waited so long for this moment...

Emotions flooded him, and he was almost afraid that this was all a dream. A wonderful, impossible dream that couldn't possibly be real.

His throat dry, his eyes moist, he drank in the sight of her. Bonnie. His little girl. He'd finally found her.

Hand trembling, he reached out and stroked the silken hair. It'd grown so long, so straight. Where were the soft little curls he remembered? The words were barely audible when he finally spoke. "Oh, Bonnie, Bonnie, do you know who I am?"

"You're my daddy." Tears flowed down the small face as she reached out her arms to him. Eliza transferred her to Walker. Bonnie wrapped her arms tightly around his neck, burying her face against his shoulder. "I thought I dreamed you, Daddy," she sobbed.

He stroked her hair, trying very hard not to break down. His heart shattered into a million pieces, only to be resurrected again. He had her. She was here and he had her. And he was never letting go.

For the first time in his life, he finally understood what tears of joy meant. "I'm real, baby. I'm real and I'm here and I'm taking you home."

Her heart full, Eliza stepped back and watched them. It was enough.

Eliza moved around her apartment, straightening things that didn't require straightening. She'd been doing this for quite a while, she thought ruefully.

The restlessness wouldn't leave.

She supposed it had to do with the feeling that her job was done and there was nothing to turn to. For once, there was no new case waiting.

She glanced toward the bookcase against the far wall. There were books there she'd been meaning to get to, but nothing enticed her. She'd already tried several times. The television remained dark, and the music from the radio she'd turned on in desperation fell on deaf ears.

She didn't know what to do with herself.

After the police had taken Allen and his wife away, she and Walker had flown back to Bedford with Bonnie. Jason was there to meet them, along with a squadron of other people he'd notified. News of the happy resolution to the two-year-old kidnapping case had leaked to the press. The airport terminal was filled to overflowing with reporters, all wanting to share the upbeat feeling of the child's homecoming.

Jason, Walker's sister, Patrice, and a host of people

Eliza didn't know, all surrounded him, shouting congratulations and questions.

That was when she'd quietly slipped away.

Her job done, she didn't want to hang around so that the news media could play up her so-called gift. She'd had enough of that. Eliza knew she was on the outside again, and tried to make her peace with it.

Except that this time, it wasn't as easy as it had become. Now being on the outside felt as lonely, as isolating as it had in the early years. The layers she'd wrapped around herself over time were all gone. Walker had made them dissolve.

So she dusted and cleaned and scrubbed and prayed for the feeling to leave.

It didn't.

There was nothing else for her to do. She was just going to have to wait this feeling out, she decided. And hope that something came up soon at the agency to keep her occupied.

The knock on the door surprised her. She wasn't expecting anyone.

The person on the other side surprised her more.

Walker crossed her threshold.

God, but he had missed her, he thought with wonder. He hadn't thought he could miss a woman as much as he had missed Eliza these past couple of days. It was all he could do not to sweep her into his arms and kiss her.

"You looked surprised to see me."

She lifted her shoulder in a half shrug, feeling almost self-conscious. What was he doing here? "I didn't expect you. How's Bonnie?"

"She's fine. She's with my sister right now. It'll take a while for her to get used to things and feel safe again, to understand why her mother isn't around. But I think we'll manage. With some help," he added, looking at her.

"You mean like a therapist? That might not be a bad idea."

"No, more like someone kind and understanding. Who could relate to her. Who felt her pain."

"You mean me."

"I mean you." He took her hands in his. "Maybe this is a lot to ask... Maybe all of it is."

"All?"

Frustrated, he blew out a breath. It wasn't supposed to come out like this, like a tangled skein of words. "I'm getting ahead of myself." He looked at her ruefully. "Maybe I should have written this down and practiced it. But how do you practice laying your heart bare?"

"Your heart?" she echoed, afraid to think, afraid to hope.

This was getting worse and worse. He retreated for a second, to gather his thoughts. To make this come out right. "Where did you disappear to at the airport?"

She shrugged, looking away. "I just stepped back. I didn't want to get in the way."

"In the way?" He stared at her incredulously. "You're the reason everything happened."

Why was he making this so difficult for her? Why couldn't he just go and move on with his life the way she knew he was going to? "Yes, but it happened, so I wasn't necessary any longer."

What was she talking about? Walker caught her hand, making her look at him. "You make yourself sound like some kind of inanimate object, a tool."

Eliza sighed. He wasn't that far off, she supposed. "Well, in a way—"

He cut her off. "In *no* way." Realizing his voice had become sharp, he softened it. "Eliza, you're not a tool, you're a person. Not an ordinary person—" he began.

"Don't meet many clairvoyants these days," she quipped.

He wasn't going to allow her to make light of this. "It's not your clairvoyance that makes you extraordinary—" Stopping, Walker looked at her closely. "And right now, that seems to be on the fritz, I'd say."

She'd had no idea he was coming here, he realized. No idea that he'd seek her out. And apparently, from the uncertain look in her eyes, she didn't know what he was about to say now, either.

That made him feel a whole lot better, as if the ground beneath him had suddenly turned solid. He'd given them both two days to try to sort things out, to let everything calm down. For the dust to settle, so to speak. All it had done for him was make him miss her more. And pray that it had done the same for her.

"You really can't tell your own future, can you? That is, your future if you agree," he clarified.

Uncertainty gave way to complete confusion. Eliza cocked her head. "Agree?"

Damn, but he wished he were more eloquent. "I know I'm saying this as if it were some merger acquisition, but—" he took her hand in his "—in my own clumsy way, I'm asking you to marry me." He laughed shortly. "I guess you can take the man away from business, but you can't take the business out of the man."

The pieces were beginning to come together, but she was afraid that she was seeing what she wanted to see. What she was praying to see.

"Does that mean that you mean business?" Eliza's voice was hardly above a whisper.

He grinned. "Never meant it more in my life, Princess Moonflower." He got a kick out of that, out of trying to imagine what she'd been like as a little girl, slipping into imaginary places in her mind.

And then the grin faded as he became serious. "You've already connected with my daughter and you've made me realize that you're the other half of my soul, Eliza. You're what's been missing all these years. Now that I've found you, I don't want to let you go. Bonnie is going to need someone like you in her life, to help her get over the hurdles. And so am I. A lifetime of hurdles. I love you, Eliza. I want you in my life on whatever terms you want to lay down. The last two days have been hell without you and I don't want to relive that again. Ever.''

Tears came to her eyes. ''You just said exactly what I was thinking about you.''

''See? We belong together.'' He brought each of her hands to his lips, kissing them one at a time. ''Say yes, Eliza, say yes.''

''You read my mind again.''

And then she kissed him, because she had read his.

* * * * *

*Be sure to look for the next book
from Marie Ferrarella. Don't miss*

ROUGH AROUND THE EDGES,

*available in March 2001 from
Silhouette Romance.*

Silhouette

INTIMATE MOMENTS™

presents a riveting 12-book continuity series:

a Year of loving dangerously

Where passion rules and nothing is what it seems...

When dishonor threatens a top-secret agency, the brave
men and women of SPEAR are prepared to risk it all as they
put their lives—and their hearts—on the line.

Available March 2001:

THE ENEMY'S DAUGHTER
by Linda Turner

When undercover SPEAR agent Russell Devane arrived at the
Pear Tree cattle station deep in the Australian outback, he had every
intention of getting close to the enemy's daughter. But all the rules
changed when Russell found himself fighting a forbidden attraction
to the breathtakingly beautiful Lise. Would he be able to capture
an evil traitor without forfeiting the love of a lifetime?

*Available only from Silhouette Intimate Moments
at your favorite retail outlet.*

Silhouette®

Where love comes alive™

Visit Silhouette at www.eHarlequin.com   SIMAYOLD10

Silhouette® —

where love comes alive—online...

eHARLEQUIN.com

your romantic life

━Romance 101━
♥ Guides to romance, dating and flirting.

━Dr. Romance ━
♥ Get romance advice and tips from
our expert, Dr. Romance.

━Recipes for Romance━
♥ How to plan romantic meals for you
and your sweetie.

━Daily Love Dose━
♥ Tips on how to keep the romance
alive every day.

━Tales from the Heart━
♥ Discuss romantic dilemmas with other
members in our Tales from the Heart
message board.

Every mother wants to see her children marry
and have little ones of their own.

One mother decided to take matters into
her own hands....

Now three Texas-born brothers are about to discover
that mother knows best: A strong man *does* need a
good woman. And babies make a forever family!

Matters of the Heart

A Mother's Day collection of
three **brand-new** stories by

Pamela Morsi
Ann Major
Annette Broadrick

Available in April at your favorite retail outlets,
only from Silhouette Books!

Silhouette®
Where love comes alive™

#1 *New York Times* bestselling author

NORA ROBERTS

brings you more of the loyal and loving,
tempestuous and tantalizing Stanislaski family.

Coming in February 2001

The Stanislaski Sisters

Natasha and Rachel

Though raised in the Old World traditions of their
family, fiery Natasha Stanislaski and cool, classy
Rachel Stanislaski are ready for a *new* world of love....

*And also available in February 2001 from
Silhouette Special Edition, the newest book in the
heartwarming Stanislaski saga*

CONSIDERING KATE

Natasha and Spencer Kimball's daughter Kate turns her
back on old dreams and returns to her hometown, where
she finds the *man* of her dreams.

Available at your favorite retail outlet.

Where love comes alive™